# RYAN

## BACKSTAGE SERIES

I0551602

### DANI RENÉ

Copyright © 2017 by Dani René
Published by Dani René
eBook ISBN: 978-0-639-90010-0
Paperback ISN: 978-0-6398104-8-5

All rights reserved, including the right to reproduce this book or portions thereof in any form whatsoever.

The following story contains mature themes, strong language, and sexual situations. It is intended for adult readers.

No part of this book may be reproduced or transmitted in any form or by any means, electronic or mechanical, including photocopying, recording, or by any information storage and retrieval system, without permission in writing. If you would like to share this book with another person, please purchase an additional copy for each recipient. If you're reading this book and did not purchase it, or it was not purchased for your enjoyment only, then please purchase your own copy. Thank you for respecting the hard work of this author.

This book is a work of fiction. Names, characters, places, and incidents either are products of the author's imagination or are used fictitiously. Any resemblance to actual events or locales or persons, living or dead, is entirely coincidental.

The author acknowledges the trademarked status and trademark owners of various products referenced in the work of fiction, which have been used without permission. The publication/use of these trademarks is not authorized, associated with, or sponsored by the trademark owner.

# DEDICATION

*To those of you too scared to show your true self to someone, don't be. For those who have ever felt, not good enough, don't. We're all perfect in our own unique imperfections.*

*Never be afraid to let you heart beat. Never be afraid to smile at that guy in the coffee shop, to take a chance and say hello. Don't ever let your fear overrule your want. That girl on the sidewalk waiting for the bus, might be waiting for you.*

*Emotions. Feelings. Affection. Love.*
*Allow it to take you. Envelop you.*
*Make you feel real.*
*It's not easy, but it's so damn worth it!*

# PROLOGUE

Choices. Decisions.

There comes a point in everyone's life where they stare at the road ahead, a path that leads two ways. To fulfill your aspirations, or to follow the direction that's set out for you by somebody else. Whether it's your family, or a partner.

My choice came almost ten years ago when I turned twenty-five. I left home and everything else behind for a chance at stardom. To fulfill my dream. But nothing prepares you for having to make a decision at the fork that lies ahead of you in your lifetime. When you need to decide—left or right.

I don't have a family anymore. They didn't understand me needing to live my own life and work toward something that I longed for. Isn't family expected to support you and your dreams no questions asked? Mine didn't. They expected I would follow in my father's footsteps, to become a lawyer. That was instilled in me from a young age. I wasn't asked what I wanted to do. I had been instructed as to what I had to do. To take over the family business and instead, I packed a backpack, grabbed my guitar and walked out.

All the possessions that he threatened to take away—all the cars, houses, holidays— everything I grew up with is now gone. Until two brothers gave me a chance, they gave me the family that had so easily left me to fend for myself. They supported not only me, but my dream, making sure I surpassed my expectations and succeeded.

Ten years later I find myself sitting in the studio working on our newest album and I still can't believe that I made my dreams a reality. All those things my father ripped from my life, I don't need, because now I have more than I ever did before and it sets my soul at ease. Most importantly, happiness.

Glancing up, I look at the girl that stole my heart ten years ago when I first walked into the audition. Callum's assistant, Kierra Thorne. Beautiful, feisty, and so goddamn sexy she has no idea how much my life changed since I met her. Although both Hayes brothers learned about my feelings for her a long time ago. It's only recently at Callum's wedding that I finally took a chance and kissed her. Needless to say the kiss turned into one incredible night. She fit so perfectly in my arms. I fit so perfectly inside her body. But, that's where it ended.

We didn't even have a chance to start before she told me that we're better off friends. The only problem is; I can't just be her friend anymore. I'm done sitting back, accepting the friend-zone bullshit. Not when I know how good it feels to have her body against mine. To see her face when she finds pleasure in my touch. I want her and after talking to Cal and Liam, knowing they support our relationship, I will make sure she doesn't walk away.

She's about to leave for the airport and I am driving her there because that's what friends do. I'm prepared. This time I will tell her everything she needs to hear and when she steps on that plane she'll know my true feelings.

The month she'll be at home will give her time to think things through. If she fights me on this, she better be ready for a war, because I am not giving up on her. I know her emotions run deep, as deep as mine, and she's going to have to get over her fear because I am not going anywhere. My heart hurts as I watch her grab her bag, shrug on her jacket, because she's flying thousands of miles away and I'll feel her absence. It will be the furthest we've ever been from each other and for this reason, unease settles in my gut. But she will come back to me.

She will be mine. I will make sure of it.

Why?

Because I'm Ryan fucking Callahan.

# RYAN

"Are you ready Ki?" Glancing at her, I can see she's nervous and I can't help wondering if she's not happy to go home, or if she's just going to miss us. My heart wants the latter, but for some reason I know it's about her family. Granted, she's never spoken about them much, all I know is that her mom passed away years ago and she grew up with her dad playing the part of both parents.

"Yes, I just need to check on Tay before we leave." She leaves me with a shy smile and heads to the office. Since Tayla fell pregnant, Callum has been watching her like a hawk, it's sweet, but I can tell that she's had enough. She's going to be taking over Kierra's job for a while, handling the admin for the band, but we can all see she's bored out of her mind.

My best friend's wife is a doer, she needs to be active, running around after the crew, making sure the sound techs are doing what they need to. For her to sit idle in front of a computer screen must be driving her stir crazy.

"You going to tell her, man?" Turning to find Liam, I nod. We've had this discussion, he knows how I feel and has been pushing me to make my move for years, but each time I try, she pushes back. I wanted to respect her feelings, to allow her time, but this is where it ends because she's mine. "There's no time like the present, brother." He chuckles leaving me glaring at his back.

Since Emma agreed to marry him, he thinks he knows everything about relationships. When I turn back to Kierra, I can't help but agree with him. There is no time like the present and today that woman is going to know exactly how I feel.

When she steps up to me, the scent of her perfume engulfs me, dragging me into her orbit. It's as if she's already a part of me, inside my bloodstream, keeping my heart pumping. "I'm ready," she murmurs quietly, she's normally feisty, but at the moment, her body is tense and all I want to do is take her to the music room and slide into her, easing the tension from her body.

Grabbing my keys, I glance at the entrance to the kitchen. "Be back in a bit," I holler and Liam gives me a salute as he sips his coffee. Other than that he offers me nothing more. There's not much to say, I slept with my best friend, I've seen her naked and the vision is ingrained in my mind. I've loved her for as long as I've known her. Fear has always been something that's held me back. With my music. With her.

Following Ki up the stairs to my Range Rover, I push the button on the key fob to unlock the car. She's been in my passenger seat so many times, but somehow this feels different. It is.

I lug her suitcase into the trunk and round the car. Once I'm in the driver's seat, I glance at her. There's so much emotion in her eyes I want to lean in and claim her lips, but she asked for friendship, which I'm giving her, for now. When we arrived back from Callum and Tay's wedding, she told me she couldn't promise me forever. I thought right then that we were over, but all she said was she needed time. I could give her time, but eventually, that will run out then she'll no longer be able to hide behind those high walls she's put up.

That night, I went to bed and my heart hurt, it was a physical ache that I never want to feel again.

With Liam's help, I've got a plan. We've set up all my tracks over the past few weeks and I'm not needed for a while, which leaves me with much needed time off. And what Ki doesn't know is that as soon as our last show is over, I'll be following her stubborn ass. She needs support and I'm going to give it to her.

Since she refused using Callum's offer of the jet, she's booked in first class on a flight that will take her far from Los Angeles, but I'll be right behind her. One month. That's all the time she's getting. Even though it's going to kill me, I'll respect her wishes for time. After that month is up, I'm going to get her. I don't care what she says.

If I told her I wanted to accompany her, she'd refuse, so I'm having to do it this way. I'm done sitting back watching her from the sidelines. She's mine, and I'm going to lay my claim. This woman will be bound to me for life.

She'll wear my ring, take my name, and be mine forever.

Whatever she's hiding, she should realize I'm not leaving, not walking away.

I know I love her, I've known it for a long time and to have her up and leave is not an option. "Are you looking forward to going home and seeing your dad?" I question as we weave through the traffic.

"I suppose so, there's not much there for me anymore, but there are things I need to…" Shaking her head as if ridding it of a bad memory, she continues, "there's unfinished business that I need to get through and my father is going to help me. He's…" She cuts a glance to me and I can feel her stare burning into the side of my face with an intensity of a flame. Whenever she looks at me I feel every emotion she's trying to convey. I wonder if she realizes that we have such an innate connection.

"He's?"

"Nothing. I will be back soon. Things will be easier once I've done this," she whispers on a sigh and everything in my head screams at me to stop the car and force her to tell me. But Kierra isn't a push over. She's a stubborn woman and if I so much as show any forcefulness for her to give more than she's willing, she'll shut down even more.

Dragging my gaze to hers, I find sadness marring her beautiful face. Her wavy hair hangs over her shoulders, it's a rich chocolate with golden highlights. She had it done for the wedding and I love how the lush color shimmers when she shakes her head, or the light catches it just right. Her normally teal eyes shine with a soft gray-blue today and it looks like the sky on a cloudy day.

Her lips are soft, plump, and glossy. She doesn't wear make-up, but she dabs a shimmery gloss on them which makes them look like edible candies. And God knows I'd love to taste them again. "What will be easier, Ki? Me and you?"

The eagerness in my voice doesn't go unnoticed.

"Ryan—"

"Sorry, I just thought—" I wave my hand, but she interrupts me.

"It's okay, I don't want to promise you something that I may not be able to keep." It's in that moment I know how it feels to have your heart ripped from your chest. Because her words do just that. They settle with a heaviness in the car and I swallow the lump in my throat.

A woman has never made me cry.

A woman has never made me beg.

And a woman has never made me love.

But she has and since we've finally had our one night, she's leaving, and fear tugs at me that she may never come back. That is the one thing that I know would destroy me.

Because as soon as she boards that flight, she'll be taking my heart along with her. And I know, I have no choice in the matter, because she owns me. She has ever since I first laid eyes on her.

We drive in silence because I can't say more. The lump in my throat threatens to suffocate me. Choking me, cutting off all the air, the same air that's thick with emotion so malevolent it's like a force swirling around us.

When people tell you love is dangerous, they're not lying. Love hurts, but deep down, I'm not giving up on her, so the pain will only last so long. Once I'm in Australia with her, she'll forget everything that's ever hurt her, she'll know I'm serious. And that's what I'm vying for.

# KIERRA

Having to lie to Callum and Liam wasn't easy. Telling Tayla and Emma the story I fabricated was difficult. But to look into Ryan's dark eyes, telling him something so far from the truth hurt me more. I know by keeping this from him for now won't hurt him. The only thing I didn't lie about was that I couldn't promise him forever. Not yet anyway.

As I step onto the plane, I'm escorted into first class. Cal made sure he upgraded me so I had the best seat. My flight from Los Angeles to Hong Kong will be shorter than I expected, and then I fly on from Hong Kong to Sydney.

With a soft sigh, I settle back, and glance out the window wishing Ryan was here. The need to wave goodbye tugs at my heart, but to be honest, I'm not sure I want to say the fateful word. Even though he drove me to the airport, we didn't say it, all we promised each other was a see you later.

I doubt I'll be back for a while. With all the doctors' visits I need to do, I'm both scared and apprehensive. There are things I ran from, now it's time to figure out what I want to do. A decision I put away, hiding it in the back of my mind, but I realize it's unavoidable now.

There's another thing that scares me about going back, and that's seeing the man who hurt me beyond compare. The only thing I'm looking forward to is seeing my dad.

When I left, he was the only person I missed, the one man I'd love and trust forever, besides my brothers for all intents and purposes, Callum and Liam. Then there's my love for Ryan. The thought startles me, but it shouldn't. There's no doubt I love him, I'd fallen for him since he ambled into the interview that day. When he smiled, my heart leaped into my throat. I blushed. The girl who was more tomboy than princess blushed for a boy in his ripped jeans and tatty T-shirt. The one with the guitar and a talent on the keyboard.

Watching him play is hypnotic. His fingers know where every key is without needing his brain to tell them where to go. The melodies he creates either tug at the heart, or make you want to dance, sway, and just enjoy life. That's Ryan. The joker of the group. But in his heart, he holds love and happiness, so infinite you can't imagine seeing him angry.

As the plane takes off down the runway, I imagine walking into the house and seeing my dad. It's been too long, getting to give him a cuddle is what I'm looking forward to. I've missed him over the years. When I first left, it was difficult. The hardest thing I'd ever had to do. So much so I spent day in and day out on the phone with him. My bill is generally through the roof, but just to hear my father be strong for me was enough to push me to live my life. He always told me how proud he was. How I was just like her.

My mother.

Closing my eyes, I rest my head and let sleep overtake me.

*The sadness that wracked me today was more than I could handle. After finding out about my mother's illness, I knew it would one day come, the choice I had to make. How can I choose something that will forever change my life? I'm only twenty.*

*As I walk into the house, I flip on the switch and drop my bag on the table in the hallway. We've just moved into this apartment. It's bigger than I wanted, but Josh said he could afford it. He has a well-paying job, but he's spent more time at his office than he has at the apartment.*

*Making my way into the kitchen, I find it dark. Perhaps he's working on a case. Since he made partner at the law firm he's been inundated with high profile cases and our relationship has been non-existent. It's taken a backseat to his high-flying career, and the so-called friends he now hangs out with.*

*Don't get me wrong, I'm proud of him, but*

it hurts. I don't want to complain, but it's lonely without him.

I need to talk to him about the offer I got today. When I stepped into the office today, I was asked to make notes in the meeting with well-known rock band Hunters in Oblivion.

As a public relations intern, I jumped at the chance. Not only to meet them, but to listen to what their plans were for their upcoming Australian tour.

After the meeting, I spoke to Callum, the lead singer, and he came right out and asked me to tour with them as assistant to the band and hopefully promoted on to their head of PR. I was in shock, but I asked him for a day to think about it.

I want to accept, it's the perfect opportunity to get my name into the music business. After the operation, I can fly to LA and start work. No doubt Josh will be angry, I know it. He hates when I have anything remotely exciting happening in my life. As if he wants me at home pregnant with his kids.

I grab a bottle of water, gulping down half before heading into our bedroom.

*When I step into the oversized room I glance around, there are clothes scattered all over the floor. Why the fuck can't he clean up after himself? It's then I hear a giggle. Not a masculine one. Once I push open the door to our en suite, I find two blonde bimbos giggling with Josh while he sucks on their fake tits.*

*He doesn't notice me, it's one of the girls who sees me first. Her gasp has him glancing up and I notice the darkness in his eyes. His pupils are dilated, and his sway tells me all I need to know. He's high. "Kitty kat," the nickname sends me spiraling.*

*How dare he call me that while he's fucking two whores?*

*I shove my way back out of the bathroom, I run into the hallway and grab my bag. "Kierra!" He calls after me, but I'm already at the door.*

*"Fuck you, Josh!"*

The rattle of the trolley jars me from the dream of the day my world shattered for the second time. That wasn't the last I saw of him.

He tried getting me back. Apologizing.

Flowers. Gifts. Everything went into the trash. They say there's a thin line between loving someone and hating them, Josh found out just how quickly I leaped over the proverbial line. There was nothing he could do to get me back over it.

"Can I get you anything?" A smooth, sultry voice pulls me from the memory.

"Red wine, please? Merlot if you have it. Bring me two of those little bottles." I smile at the stewardess and she nods. I'm not going anywhere, might as well drink my sorrows away.

When my mind drifts back to Ryan, I wonder if the ache in my chest matches the one in his. The night we spent together he told me whenever we're apart it hurts. At the time, I thought he was joking, making fun of me. But now I'm flying thousands of miles away, I know what he meant.

The stewardess returns and leaves both bottles for me, I open one and fill the plastic glass. I'm not used to travelling like this anymore, I'm normally on the private plane with the boys. This is nice. Spacious. The only thing missing is Ryan. There's so much I wanted to tell him before I left, but it's best to leave it until I get back. Until I am sure my health isn't a concern and I can explore a long-term relationship.

Sipping my wine, I pull out my laptop and open the lid. Even though I should be on holiday, I need to check my emails, write press releases, and make sure the band are confirmed for their upcoming appearances and Tayla has everything she needs while I'm away. As much as Tay is trying to help, Callum is being overly protective of her. With a baby on the way, he's been more of a pain in the ass than normal. I can't help smiling at the way he cares for her, but I can also see how annoyed she is at his insistence she stays home all the time. He's always been a loner, he'd fuck women, but I didn't think I'd ever see him married with a baby on the way.

Liam is different, as much as he loves Emma, I can see how he still struggles at times. She's an incredible support to him. Accepting a man with so many dark demons hanging around must be difficult, I know I'd find it stressful, but that little brunette is a perfect match for our drummer.

I wouldn't be surprised to arrive back to news that Emma is pregnant. Liam has a sort of caveman way of doing things. When we're out and a man so much as looks at Emm, it's as if he's ready to kill. Suddenly, as I sip my wine, I miss them. My family.

And then there's Ryan. My sweet, caring man. He's everything a woman could want. Attentive, romantic, funny, and after one incredible night together, he's an amazing lover. His body isn't chiseled or cut like most of these rock stars, but he's beautifully built. He looks after himself and the smooth toned torso that set my body alight with hunger is perfect to me.

Those dark cocoa eyes that melt when I walk into the room, the smile that lights up both his face and any room he's in is how he stole my heart. He walked in and grinned at me and I was a goner. There was no chance for my heart. He was it. And somehow, he thinks I'm it for him. All I have to do is make sure I'm ready to be in a long-term relationship. This trip with be the deciding factor.

Not long after I finish my wine—both bottles—I feel exhaustion hit, I know I have a layover, but I sit back and close my eyes, anyway.

# RYAN

"When are you leaving?" I turn to regard Callum. Even though he's older than me by a few years, I feel as if we're equals.

"After the show, I told you I'm not leaving before that. Also, she's asked for time. Which I'll give her. I asked Demitri to be ready, I'll confirm the time. I've already packed," I chuckle. "All I need to do is make sure the apartment will be taken care of while I'm away," I shrug. If I could've left today, I would've. Four pairs of eyes are burning into me and they're all excited for what I'm about to do. "What if she doesn't want me there?" I suddenly question.

They all stare at me as if I've grown another limb. Cal, his wife Tayla, Liam, and his fiancée Emma. A set of brothers, and a set of sisters. As much as I want to believe Ki feels the same, she's pushed more times than I've pulled and I'm not sure if this is a good idea. Doubt is a motherfucker.

"Look, Ryan, you know I love you like a brother." Tayla pushes up from the chair and rubs her belly in slow circles. She's five months pregnant and they're about to go find out the sex. Her serious expression has me smirking because I know I'm in for it. She's a feisty woman, both sisters are, but I know that's why my best friend loves her. "She may not know it yet, but she loves you. And there's nothing more romantic than a man willing to travel across the world to see you."

Callum clears his throat and I can't help chuckling. "Is that so, Petal?" She blushes at his nickname and he pulls her into his arms.

"Oh God, can you two keep your hands off each other for ten fucking seconds." Liam growls in frustration and Emma, who's perched on his lap giggles.

"Shut it, take your fiancée out or something and stop raining on my parade."

Callum's retort comes quickly.

"Okay kids, enough. Cal, take your woman to get her scan, we want to know if we're buying pink or blue." I chuckle at his indignant face.

"Come on, Petal. See you later guys." As soon as they're out of the room Liam stares at me and I know he's about to give me shit. He wants me to go after Ki, and as much as I'm doubting myself and coming up with excuses not to, I have a feeling I'm about to get the talking to of my life, so I nod before he can say anything more.

"I'll go." I murmur, "I swear, as soon as I step off the stage I'll head straight for the airport." Lifting my gaze, I meet both Emma and Liam's stares. Both nod and smirk.

"Go get her, Ryan. I know she loves you," Emm's sweet voice makes me smile as she rises and pads over to me. I nod, leaning in to give her a cuddle. Her soft scent of peaches is clear and I know that's only one reason why Liam calls her Peach. Any other, I'd rather not know.

Once she leaves us, I regard my brother

from another mother and he smirks. "You know you're going to come back here and there's going to be a shiny diamond on her ring finger?" He quips confidently. I have no answer to that. All I can do is shrug and hope he's right.

"I'm Ryan Callahan," I rasp and her cheeks darken with a soft rosy hue. It's the most beautiful thing I've ever seen.

"I'm Kierra, I'm Callum's assistant. He's just finishing up a meeting, but you're welcome to wait." Her voice with her Australian accent, it's like a melody I'm not sure I'd ever tire of. Her button nose, with those full rosy lips and wide eyes make for a beautiful woman. With those beautiful golden-brown waves that hang to the middle of her back she looks angelic. Her skin is lightly tanned. Almost golden giving her an ethereal glow. Deep soulful eyes, the color of a stormy sky peek at me under thick lashes.

"I'd wait anywhere you are," my cocky response earns me a smile, her cheeks have the most incredible set of dimples I've ever seen. This woman is perfect. Her face is innocent, yet serious, her eyes betray agony, but offer kindness, and her mouth is tempting, it looks good enough to devour.

"Can I get you a coffee? The guys will be out to see you soon," she responds, her cute button nose scrunches when she smiles. Jesus, I need to focus.

"Yes, coffee would be good." She doesn't wait for me to say anything more before turning on her heel and stalking toward an open doorway. Before I can follow a door behind me swings open and I'm met with the blue eyes of Callum Hayes. Playboy and rock star.

"Ryan?" He questions and all I can do is nod. I'm awestruck. I've seen him in concert so many times. I've seen him on the front page of tabloids, newspapers, and every time I have, he's been nothing but gracious. Even now, as I stand here a newbie to this world, he offers me his hand and a grin.

"Yes, it's good to meet you," I manage to get out before he releases my hand to say goodbye to the man dressed in a suit and tie. Once the man has left, Callum turns to me and nods.

"Let's get you in there," he grins that boyish smile I know most girls drool over and I follow him into the studio. The room is small but comfortable with equipment lying around. He settles himself on the sofa and gestures toward a keyboard and guitar which is set up, ready to be played. "I know you're well versed in both, let me hear what you can do."

"Thank you, yes," nerves kick in as I settle myself in front of the keyboard which is what I'm auditioning for, the role of keyboardist for the band. With the sweetest voice in my head that I can't shake of the girl I just met, I've got a melody in mind. Getting my fingers ready, I inhale a deep breath. It's state of the art, and I can't wait to feel the keys beneath my touch. It's like a woman, you have to caress it, stroke it, and make it sing for you. Much like I'd love to do to Kierra.

As soon as my fingers rest on the keys, my eyes flutter closed and I get lost inside my head. The melody echoes around us and all I feel are the notes. Everything is in tune, and I hit every note, I feel every part of the song.

Everything is lost, there's only me and song.

*Slow, haunting, and melodic, I play "Nothing Else Matters" by Metallica like I was born to. As I reach the final notes, my eyes open and I find both Callum and Kierra, along with Liam, the older Hayes brother gawking at me.*

*Before I can say anything, Liam steps forward and smirks at me and asks the question that I've been working toward all my life, "when can you start?"*

# KIERRA

I sigh as I step into the house I used to call home—the place I grew up in. Nothing's changed and the memories of what I went through flood my mind. I wish I was happy to be back, but the reason I'm here doesn't bring me joy. As soon as the door shuts, I hear dad. "Baby girl? Is that you?" He comes bounding into the hallway. He'd offered to pick me up at the airport, but I know how long the drive is and I don't want him sitting in the car for that long. His health hasn't been the best, so I'd rather know he was safe, so I told him not to worry. I am more than capable of getting home. "Oh my God, you're so beautiful." The tears in his eyes glisten and I realize me leaving home hurt him. When I flew to LA and told him I'm not coming back crushed him.

"Hey dad," as old as I am, I'll always be a baby to him. My heart hurts, I miss him more than I imagined I would. All I wanted was to escape. Run away from my life, and in the process cut myself off from everyone. My family.

"I'm so happy to see you." His arms are warm, filled with love and I try not to think about why I'm here. I've been putting it off for too long and now is the time to decide what I want to do. The house is still the same as my dad walks me into the kitchen. "Did you have a good flight, honey?"

"Yes, I'd forgotten how long it is. What's worse is the cab ride home, it's about as long as the flight," I giggle. "I'm feeling jet lagged, but I think a good night's sleep will help." He nods with a smile filled with love. He's the only person who knows I'm back and I would like to keep it that way. There isn't anyone else that I want to face and as soon as I can, I want to go back home, back to LA.

"Well, why don't you go ahead and relax,

I've booked a table at a new restaurant down the road, it's got everything from burgers to sushi. I know you're a fan." My father hates cooking, that was always mom's job. I remember when she first died, Dad tried making a pasta dish. It had burnt so badly—sticking to the pot. We tried to salvage some of it, but it ended up in the trash, along with the steel pot.

"That sounds good, thanks dad."

Heading down the hallway to my old bedroom, I feel nostalgia hit and smile at the fact that it's not changed since I left. That was the day I walked out and got on a plane, a one-way ticket, and didn't look back. The agony of leaving behind something precious forced me to never look into the past, to never allow myself to feel the emptiness that came with what I had to do.

When you're not given a choice in life it's hard to come to terms with the decision. But this was life or death, so I chose life. Who in their right mind would choose death?

The restaurant is quiet, thankfully, but I can't help glancing around. I'm not sure if Josh still lives close by, but the apartment I'd left him in is only a block away. I hope I don't see him because after the way we left things, I can't stomach the agony that man brings me. After the day I caught him cheating, he'd begged and pleaded for me to take him back, he went into rehab and cleaned himself up. But there was always distrust between us, I found myself second guessing everything he said.

I met with him a couple of times, mainly to allow him to take a step in his recovery to apologize to the people he hurt. However, I just couldn't bring myself to go back to a life with him. Like I said, I'd stepped over the line from loving him to something entirely different, and there was no going back.

Even though I knew my father was hurt and missed me, he supported my decision. He allowed his baby girl to go off into the world and make her life somewhere else. "Kierra, there's something you should know." When my father starts a sentence like that, my body shuts down. Because I recall the last time he said that. It was the last time I saw my mother healthy.

The cancer ate away at her slowly. It's the most horrific thing I've ever experienced and to have her deteriorate before my eyes was something I wouldn't wish on my worst enemy.

"What's wrong dad?" My brows furrow in confusion, concern, and worry. But there's a hint of a smile on his face and I know I'm clearly missing something.

"You know my retirement is coming up at the end of the year and I've decided to stop wallowing in the self-pity that's held me prisoner for so long." Cocking my head to the side in question, I watch my father's eyes glisten with tears. "I've been thinking of possibly moving to LA, not to intrude on your life, but to be near you, if you need me. What do you think, honey?" My parents had me young, he's only in his early fifties and he's still healthy and strong so I don't see why he shouldn't do it. It would also set my mind at ease knowing he's close by.

"I'd like that, dad. To have you nearby." His big hand engulfs mine and he gives it a squeeze. Just then, the waiter steps up to our table.

"Can I get you drinks?" His voice echoes through every part of me and my world spins on its axis. As I drag my eyes up to his I recognize him instantly. Although, he isn't the man I walked out on all those years ago. He's older. He looks like he's had a rough ten years since he said goodbye to me. "Kitty kat?" The name still makes me cold and angry.

"My name is Kierra, I'd prefer you to keep yourself professional." I bite back my retort. The man who was a high paid lawyer has fallen so low he's now serving me a drink. He also used to think he was better than everyone, treating people who didn't earn what he did like trash, and now that I look at him I can't help the satisfied smirk that curls my lips.

"Of course, Kierra. Can I get you something to drink?" There's a certain satisfaction that comes from seeing someone who's ripped you apart groveling. Does this make me a bad person? Yes, probably. But damn it feels good.

"I'll have a Chardonnay, please." Glancing at my dad, I notice him staring a little too intently at the menu and I know he's trying not to laugh. My dad was about to go and kill Josh when I told him that he'd cheated on me. So, no love lost there really.

"Bring me a whiskey on the rocks." My dad rumbles. When we're alone, he looks at me earnestly. "I didn't realize he worked here, I'm sorry honey. It's the first time I've been in here and if I'd known that asshat worked here—"

"It's okay, Dad. I can handle him. Besides, I've moved on." I tell him with a smile, only to earn one back.

"Have you met someone?" The question I've been waiting for comes and I nod. I might as well tell him about Ryan.

"There has been someone. I mean, we're not dating yet. But…" I trail off not sure how to explain it. Josh returns and my words taper off as he places our drinks on the table.

"Are you ready to order?" He questions and I can't help looking at him again. He's so much older than I remember. Time hasn't been on his side and deep down, I want to smile because of what he did to me, but on the other hand I can't bring myself to care. I've moved on, my life is so much better without him in it. Realization hits me then and there that finding him in bed with two women was a blessing. It gave me the final push to live my life and find what makes me happy.

"I'll have the salmon and tuna sushi platter, bring extra soy sauce as well," my voice is confident, not the same shy girl he remembers and his stare is as intense as the heat on a hot summers day. He nods, making a note on the pad of paper, then turns his attention to my father and waits.

"I'll have the Porterhouse steak, rare, with salad. Oh, and add fries to that," Dad says in a gruff tone. Josh nods and makes a note. Once we're alone, I know the inquisition is going to start. "So, tell me about this man?" My dad offers his loving smile and I can't help the blush that heats my cheeks when I remember Ryan's grin, his kiss, and those soulful eyes.

"It's Ryan, the keyboardist for the band, you remember last summer when you visited?" He nods, "It's been a long time coming, Dad." There are so many things I can tell my father about the man who holds my heart, but there's one thing I know will impress him. "He cares for me, Dad, there's nothing he wouldn't do for me. He's respectful and he's never ever pushed me more than I wanted to give."

"When I was there, even for the short time I spent around you, I can see the way you both look at each other. It's different to how you are with Callum and Liam. It's okay, honey. You love him, I know." He smiles and I nod.

I do. I love Ryan Callahan more than anything. And once this is over, I'll go back and I'll finally tell him how much I love him. "So much, Dad. I just hope he can give me a chance to explain why I had to come home.

It's not easy, and I haven't told him the real reason for this trip. I lied and I feel terrible about it." My confession halts and my dad sits back regarding me earnestly.

"Look, honey, there are times we omit to tell those we love something to keep from hurting them. I think you should have told him, maybe it would have given you an insight into his feelings. But, it's done now, and if he loves you as much as you do him, then I'm sure he'll see why you lied and forgive you."

"I know, but, deep down I know he would've wanted to be here with me. Supporting me through this, but I didn't want him to see me in the hospital, going through the tests and having doctors prod at me. I've put this off for too long. The moment I realized how I felt about him, I knew I had to come home and finish what I started all those years ago."

Silence hangs in the air, but it's not uncomfortable. I know my father and he's digesting what I've just told him. When he sits forward, leaning his elbows on the table, he regards me with a gentle smile. "Then finish it and go to him. No time like the present." With that the conversation moves to lighter topics and I feel myself breathe again. My heart still aches knowing what lies ahead of me for the next few weeks.

# RYAN

Two and a half weeks have passed since I let her get on a plane and fly across the world and I can't wait anymore. I know I promised her a month, but fuck, I can't live without her.

After driving both Callum and Liam crazy over the past couple of weeks, I've decided to pack my bags and go. The show we played last night was incredible, but there was one thing missing. Her.

Liam has just dropped me off at the hangar where our jet was parked, waiting and ready to take me to the woman I love.

"Mr. Callahan, good to see you again." The pilot, Demitri, offers his hand which I accept.

"You too, thank you for your assistance,"

I nod, while shaking his hand. He's been flying us around for almost seven years. One of the best pilots, along with his co-pilot, Stefan. They head into the cockpit and I settle back, ready for the long journey. I'm ready. I hope she is too.

The private jet is classic, simple, and understated. With dark blue leather seats that almost match our logo, the shiny oak veneer finish on the cabinets and small tables between the seats are of the highest quality.

I've gotten used to traveling this way, and having the plane to myself, I know it will give me time to think without disturbance from other passengers, even flying first class in a commercial plane.

When I feel the wheels propel us down the runway, it's then that I realize I'm doing something out of my comfort zone and I'm sure Ki is going to think the same thing. All I can do is hope she's willing to give us a chance. There's no doubt we belong together; I just need to make her see it. Make her accept it.

Sitting back, I shut my eyes and take a

deep inhaling breath. And as sleep lulls me, it's her I see.

"Welcome to Sydney, are you here on holiday?" The woman stamping my passport smiles. She's as tanned as Ki but her blonde hair offsets her bright green gaze.

"Yes, well, I'm here to propose to my girlfriend." Her smile only widens at the news as she hands me back the passport including a small map of the city.

"That's exciting, good luck. I'm sure she'll say yes." My heart thuds at the idea of Kierra being mine. Excitement, fear, elation, and the dreaded anxiety all swirl together in a storm raging through me. Nodding a *thank you*, I grab my suitcase head toward the exit. There in the arrivals is the driver waiting with a name plate with my pseudonym.

*I hope she'll say yes.*

There's still apprehension rippling through me. It's unwarranted, I remember how it felt being with her. We match. We're made for each other, nothing felt as right as having her in my arms. Her beautiful skin pressed against mine was like a dream come true. One that I don't want to wake from.

"Mr. Callahan?" A thick Australian accent from the driver whispers as I near him. With a swift nod, I pull out my passport for him to verify.

"Yes, I need to get to The Langham, please?" He nods and we head out to the unmarked SUV sitting in a parking spot not far from the building itself. He opens the trunk and once my suitcase is safely stored, I slip into the backseat.

We weave our way through the city as I go over the plan in my head. Her address is safely stored in my phone which I'll be using very soon. Once I get some rest I'll shower, get ready and make sure I've got the ring in my pocket.

If I wasn't so tired, I'd go to her right now. Just to see the smile on her face, to surprise her and tell her that I'll be whatever she needs me to be. To give her the support she needs. Whatever she's going through I want her to know I'm not going anywhere. I can be the man she needs. It's time she stops being so independent and stubborn.

This is the first time we'll be alone, and I mean completely alone together since the wedding. I know she has feelings for me, but will it be enough for her to finally admit it and let me in. The memory of the one night we had together is seared, ingrained in my mind.

The way her body moved against mine, her soft blue gray eyes seemed to darken as she accepted the pleasure I gave her.

*"Come on, Kiki, just let me in. One night, let's forget who we are and just be." I implore her. We're in the hotel room alone, no Hayes brother's and no Quinn sister's. Just me and Kierra. Her dress is elegant as it hugs her slight frame. Sweet and sexy, that's her.*

*I've waited, I've been patient, but slowly my desire is taking over. The need I have for her, the love that seems to make my heart swell to the point of pain is more than I can take. All I've wanted since I saw her was to kiss her, to feel her* skin on mine.

Yes, there've been other women, I've fucked around, but nothing compares to having a woman you love beneath you. I want to take her and make her moan, beg, and plead. I want her soft, melodic whimpers to play for me like a song on repeat. I want us to create music with our bodies. Melodies with our hearts, and harmonies as we both find release in each other.

"Ryan, I do want you, there's no doubt in my mind. I just think if we do this, step over the line, we'd never be able to go back. Never be friends again," her voice is resigned, confident and serious about losing our friendship, but that will never happen. This is where we were meant to be. There's no other woman I'd rather be with. She needs to know that.

"Kiki, we will always be friends. Do you hear me? And if you want to step over this line, if you want me inside you, we'll be so much more. Don't you understand? I—"

Shaking her head, she places a hand on my chest and my body sizzles with heat. With need. I was about to tell her I love her. But I realize she's not ready for it. "Ry," my name is a whisper on her soft lips. "I want you." My cock hardens in my slacks. It's time to take her and make her come, over and over again.

Without waiting, I crash my mouth on hers, I swallow each whimper as I lick into her mouth. She tastes like strawberries and champagne. Her lips are warm, soft, and pliable. My hands trail down her arms to her hips and I grip them, tugging her to me, allowing her to feel how much I need her. How badly I want her.

"Ryan, please," her words are whispered along my mouth and I inhale them, bask in them, and I reach for the zipper of her dress and tug it down. Once the soft material falls to the floor and pools at her feet, I take a step back. Both breaking the kiss and halting my breaths.

Dressed in charcoal lace panties and a bra to match, she's slim, but toned. Her breasts aren't big, but they'll fit in my hands perfectly. She's waif-like and beautiful. I can easily lift her up and throw her on the bed, but this is our first time and I want it to be perfect.

"I can take those offending items off, or you can, but I want you naked. I want to see those beautiful breasts, and I'm hungry to see that incredible pussy," my voice is raspy and her breathing hitches slightly, sending pleasurable jolts straight to my straining cock. Her hands move quickly and she unclasps her bra, allowing it to fall beside her.

Rosy taut nipples which peak under my gaze greet me and I can't stand it any longer. I lean in and lave at them. Swiping my tongue over each one and I can't stifle the groan of satisfaction that rumbles through me. "Ryan, oh, God," she whimpers which in turn only makes me suck and bite on them. Eliciting more mewls from her plump lips.

Her fingers tangle in my hair, pulling me closer, it's as if I can't get close enough, but I damn well try. Without a word, I tug her panties down and I find myself kneeling at her feet. Worshiping her from the floor. She glances down and her normally stormy eyes are pinned on me.

"Open your legs, Kiki," she spreads her thighs and I'm met with the most perfect pussy I've ever seen. Reaching up, I stroke the slick lips and her knees buck. "On the bed, lie back and let me see you," she obeys with a smile. As soon as she's on her back on those satin sheets, I unbutton my shirt, tugging it off and letting it slip to the floor. My slacks are next, leaving me in my boxer briefs. Her eyes shimmer in the low light of the moon shining through the window. Her glistening pussy is smooth, and my mouth waters to taste it. Falling to my knees, I stroke her inner thighs. A small whimper falls from her lips and I glance up to find her gaze trained on me.

With a smirk, I lean in and lick her smooth lips, reveling in the taste of this incredible woman. It feels as if I'm dreaming, but this is all real. She's real. With that thought in mind, I devour her. Opening her to my gaze, I dart my tongue inside her tight heat. Her sweetness is intoxicating, as if I've taken a hit directly to the vein. She's going to be my addiction, and I wouldn't have it any other way.

"Please, Ryan," her voice is thick with desire, needy and I don't deny her. Plunging two fingers into her, she cries out my name as she comes apart. Her thighs tremble and her body bucks off the bed as an orgasm rattles through her.

"So beautiful," my words are filled with love, as I regard her flushed cheeks, her dripping *sex, and her fingers fisting the sheets. I can't hold back any more. Rising to full height, I shove off my boxers and grab the condom from the pocket of my slacks and sheath myself.*

*Moving over her, I settle between her trembling thighs and lean in, kissing her allowing her to taste the sweetness she gifted me with. "Ryan, please don't tease me," she smiles as she licks her arousal from my lips and I slide into her.*

*"Jesus, Kiki, you're so tight." My grunt is rewarded with a giggle, and she lifts her hips to meet mine. Our bodies meet in a dance, our skin igniting need and desire, and our mouths consume each other. Her legs wrap around my waist and pull me in, as if she wants me to climb inside her, to mold myself into her being and I don't deny her. I drive in as deep as I can possibly go and realize in this moment, it will never be enough. One night will only make me want more, and I'll be damned if we lose this.*

*"Faster, please," she pleads, imploring me with a heated gaze, and I pull out, thrusting back in. Faster, and deeper. Harder and rougher and she meets me with every roll of my hips. Her body bows and I can't hold on any longer when*

*her pussy clamps down on my cock. Reaching between us, I circle her clit with my thumb and she explodes, her cries echo around us like a symphony.*

*"Ki," her name is a murmur on my lips. When our eyes meet there's an emotion that steals my breath. Love. She loves me. And with one look, I hope she can see I love her too.*

"We're here mate," the driver announces, dragging me from the memory and bringing me attention to the present.

"Thank you." I offer with a smile and open the car door. He nods and pops the trunk. As I make my way into the reception area of the hotel, I find myself doubting this decision again. It's fucking ridiculous because I know she wants me and loves me, but there's a niggling feeling deep down that keeps cropping up and I don't know if I should actually be doing this.

If the guys were here, I know they'd tell me I'm being silly and I should get my woman. They both fought long and hard to have their beautiful ladies on their arms, and this is no different. Except, I'm not used to getting what I want. I've always been scared of taking a step outside of my comfort zone, of allowing people in. She's been no different.

The thing with love is that it's not easy, it takes work and sometimes sacrifice. As I step up to the desk to check in, I realize one thing, she's worth every damn thing. All I have to do is make her see it. You see, Kierra Thorne is a difficult, stubborn woman.

"Good morning, Sir, how can I help you today?" The woman smiles up at me and I notice the recognition on her face but she doesn't say anything, thankfully.

"I'm checking in, Ryan Callahan," I slide my passport over to her and she nods, taking my identification and her bright red nails fly across the keyboard of her computer.

When she glances at me again, it's with a flawless smile. "This is your key. Do you need assistance with your luggage?"

"No, I'm fine. Thanks." Grabbing the card and my passport, I head toward the elevators. We've stayed here before while on tour, it's a luxurious hotel and I can't wait to get Ki into my room.

The elevator ride to the third floor is quick and I'm thankful nobody has recognized me yet. It's never easy traveling without our bodyguards, but it seems luck is on my side. Let's hope it holds out. As soon as I reach the suite, I head straight for the bed. Setting my alarm, I toe off my trainers and get comfortable. I'm giving myself an hour of shut eye before getting ready to go to her.

I open the suitcase and pull out my clothes I packed for this moment. When I meet her father, I don't want to come across as the grungy rocker, I want to impress him, to get his blessing to propose to his baby girl. Getting his approval will be the first step in stealing her heart. I know she loves him dearly, and if he can see how much I love her, I know she will too.

Once I've hung up the shirt and slacks,

I head into the bathroom and take in my appearance. Jet lag is a bitch, I look tired, but I'm ready to get this show on the road.

Turning on the spray, I watch as the water cascades from the showerhead and the steam fogs up the bathroom. As soon as it's piping hot, I step under the spray and moan in appreciation of the hot water as it hits my tired muscles. An hour was not long enough, but I can't waste any more time. If I don't do this now, I'll chicken out and that's going against everything I want.

The tension is running rampant through my muscles at the thought of her turning me away. *What if she's here for her ex? Does she even want me?*

These thoughts run through my mind in a loop and as much as I want to believe we're made for each other, there's always a niggling feeling that she'll walk away.

Shaking my head of those thoughts, I lather up and take deep breaths to calm myself. The spicy scent of my body wash invigorates me and I find myself rushing to get out of the shower and dressed. Once I'm back in the bedroom, my phone beeps with a message from Liam wishing me luck.

I wanted to call home, but with the time differences, I'll leave it till I know what's happening between us. With a quick text to him, I pull on my jeans and the dress shirt. Normally, I'm a jeans and T-shirt kind of guy, and wearing a button up is stifling.

I'm ready a few minutes later and heading out the door when my phone once again alerts me of a message. This time, my heart stops at the name on screen. *Kierra.*

*I just wanted to touch base and let you know I'm doing fine. It's been a whirlwind seeing my dad again. I miss LA though. Kiki*

I don't respond, instead, I make my way down to the lobby of the hotel and out to find the car waiting as I requested. I don't wait for him to get out and open the door, instead, I slip into the backseat giving him a smile. Once I've informed him of the address, he offers a swift nod and we're shooting off down the road with my heart in my throat.

When the cab pulls up outside a beautiful house with an immaculate garden, I take it in. My girls' home. The place that holds her past and those secrets she seems to hide. There's a car in the driveway and one parked on the sidewalk. "I won't be too long I don't think," I inform the driver and he nods. Opening the door, I exit the car and from the sidewalk, all seems quiet. I wonder if she's here. Perhaps she's out with friends.

Making my way up the path, I head toward the door, but hear voices coming from the side of the house. Even though I know I shouldn't be eavesdropping, I can't help following the pathway that leads to a small shed. Kierra's voice is low, but urgent, and the fear that she's in trouble sends my feet moving forward, but what I find halts me in my tracks. Inches apart from each other are Kierra and a guy I've never seen before.

"No, I told you, it was a mistake. I miss you, Kitty Kat. You've always been the one I wanted." My heart thuds painfully in my chest, and the anger, jealousy, and rage strangle me. *Say no, Ki. Please say no to him.* The words roll on repeat in my head and I hold my breath, waiting for her to push him away. For her to tell him to leave, but she doesn't. *She must have come home for him.*

She's peering up at the man who's caged her in and I can't help feeling anger surge through my veins. He leans in and their mouths are inches apart. I can't watch this anymore, but just before I walk away, he leans in further and plants a kiss on her lips.

Pain rushes through me like a tidal wave and agony grips my heart. Ten long years I've waited for her. To hold her, kiss her, to make her mine, but she's always pushed me away, and now I see why. Pivoting, I rush toward the gate when I see a man striding toward me.

"Can I help you, son?" He questions, frowning at me and I realize the recognition hasn't hit him yet. We met when he visited Ki in LA a few times, but I don't want to tell him anything more than I have to.

"No, it seems I've arrived too late." I shake my head and as we both turn to regard the couple. She's turned to face us and steel-blue eyes spark with guilt as she pushes away from the man and runs toward us.

But I can't wait, I don't want her excuses.

She's made a choice.

There's no longer me and her. She came home for him.

"Ryan." Her voice is filled with sadness and I'm sure she didn't want to see me here.

"I'll go. It seems you have your hands full." I gesture toward the man who's found a spot behind her. Before I turn to leave I offer her a smile. "Take care, Kiki."

"No! Ryan, please let me explain." She shouts behind me, but I ignore her walking past the older man and making my way back to the private car that's waiting on the opposite curb. She doesn't run after me and I don't expect her to.

It's time to go home.

# KIERRA

It's been three weeks since I stepped on a plane and left him in LA, three long weeks of test, doctor's visits, and CT scans, all of which Ryan doesn't know about. With an important appointment coming up, one that tells me what my future holds, I'm not sure I can come clean with Ryan yet.

I'm frozen in place, shock coursing through me. *What is he doing here?* I watch him walk away. Even though I should stop him I don't because I'm scared to tell him I'm half a woman. That I may not be able to give him children if ever we did get together and he wanted to spend forever with me. *How do you tell that to a man you love?*

"You should go." I turn to Josh who's been calling the house since he saw me that the restaurant. I've refused him almost every day, and of course, the day he shows up uninvited, is the same day Ryan walks in on him trying to kiss me. "I don't want you here, you've fucked my life up once before, I won't allow you to do it again." His face is one of anguish, but I don't care. He brought this on himself. When he walks away I feel nothing. The one man who took my heart when he left is gone. The car he climbed into is gone and it's taken me along with it.

I know without Ryan I'm a shell. He's had my heart since the first time I saw him. He's always been there for me and now he thinks I've come home for another man. When that can't be further from the truth.

I came back here for him. To make sure I can give him a full life.

"You should go after him, baby girl. That man loves you." My dad's deep timber rumbles behind me and I turn to find his serious expression. Shaking my head, I turn and walk back into the house. This is a huge fuck up. He shouldn't have come because then he'd never have found out. The test results would have been back tomorrow and I could have gone back without telling everyone what happened to me.

"I can't tell him, dad. How can a man want me if he knows I'll never bear children?" My dad's warm hand on my shoulder steadies me and the compassion emanating from him stirs my emotions. Tears tumble from my eyes and the pain searing my heart for what I'll never have rips me apart.

"Kierra, baby, listen to me." He spins me around and as I peer up at the man who's had to be both mother and father to me I know that he'll always give me the best advice. "If your mother had told me that she couldn't have children, I would still have married her. When you love someone, there's never a doubt in your mind that you'll want them through good and bad. That's what real love is. I can't tell you what to do, but I can advise you that the way that man looked at you was nothing short of admiration, love, and that's not something you find every day."

"Dad, I know. It's just difficult to tell him. He's known me for almost ten years and I've just never told anyone. It's been something I've shied away from. That fear of people pitying me, it drives me to work harder at not showing them the real me."

"Kierra Thorne, you're an incredible woman. Let him see you. Remember, you can't make the decision for him, he needs the chance to choose the real you. Give him that much, if you love him like I know you do, and I can see you do, then let Ryan decide if you're the girl for him." He's right, he's always right. Ryan has an idea of who I am and he seems to want me. Now he'll need to learn who the real Kierra Thorne is. The question is, would he be able to accept me as I am, or will it be too much for him to handle.

"Thanks, dad. I'll talk to him." Swiping my wet cheeks, I glance at the man who I've looked up to all my life. His heart is still broken from when we lost mom, but he's fought and got on with his life. Now it's time for me to do the same.

"Good girl. I'm going to get dinner going, you need to go after your man." He winks and leaves me in the living room with my heart in my hands. I'm about to do something that will change my life, I'm going to be honest with the man I love.

I should have told him years ago. The reason I kept pushing him away was only because I wasn't sure if my health would give me a forever with him. I love him. I've always known it. I've just never had the courage to tell him. That's about to change.

As I head out, I plant a kiss on my dad's cheek. "Thanks for everything." He peers up at me with similar eyes to mine.

"Honey, just remember, if he can't accept you at your worst, he's not good enough to get your best." My father, ever the romantic.

"I know dad. I'm going to let him decide and if he doesn't want to walk this line with me, then I'll let go. It just hurts to think about that option."

He nods, understanding painting his features. "It will hurt because you love him. It's not an easy emotion to tamper down. Love is wild and free, it's something that could burn you alive, but it's also something that can keep you living."

"He does. There's been many days where Ryan has given me breath to live, to get through the day. I've just never had the courage to tell him." Tears prick my eyes, but I blink them back. My heart hurts. I can't lose him.

"Kierra, it's time you tell him then. You shouldn't be scared, let your heart guide you, but let your head keep you on the road, don't veer off and change yourself for a man, let him accept you as you are. Give him your truth and he'll love you more for it."

I nod because words don't come to me. There's too much pain, elation, sadness, and anger swirling through me.

"I'm going to make it right." He nods and pulls me in for a bear hug. My father always gave the best hugs. He reminds me of Liam. Strong arms that seem to hold you up when you want to fall. Liam's been like a big brother to me most of my adult life and I wish he was here now to give me some advice on his best friend.

"Good girl. Now go get your man."

As I rush to the car, I mull the explanation

around in my mind. How I'm going to tell Ryan the truth. What Dad said made me see that I've always put my life on hold because of what happened to my mom. But when I stopped living, so did my dreams. I've always wanted a family, and when they told me I may never get that chance it felt as if I'd been cheated.

I lived with anger toward the thing that stole my mother. Cancer. The dreaded C word that no one wants to hear. So here I am, pulling on a skirt and blouse hoping to go and explain everything to the man I want to spend the rest of my life with.

All I can do is hope he understands and forgives me for running. That when he hears the real reason that I'm here it doesn't scare him off. It's not easy losing someone you love. I've seen my father live through it and I don't want to put Ryan through it. But ultimately, it's his choice.

He needs to have all the cards on the table and make a choice. I've had mine made for me when I was younger and it feels as if your freewill is stolen, robbed. And I shouldn't do that to him. As I drive down the road, I hit dial on my phone, and when Ryan answers, my heart catapults into my throat.

"Hi."

"Ryan, where are you? The Radisson Blu?" My voice us urgent, filled with fear that he'll tell me he's on the jet back to LA.

"Yeah." I don't blame him for being angry.

"Stay there, I'm on my way." With that, I hang up and pray I'm not too late to make him see, to give him the truth.

# RYAN

When she called moments ago I feared the worst, but since she's on her way, I might as well give her the benefit of the doubt. To allow her a chance to explain what she's doing here. Perhaps it is a mistake and she's coming here to tell me she's moved on. But I need to hear it from her.

The knock on the door sends my blood pressure skyrocketing. "Hi," I step aside and let her into the room. She's dressed in a beautiful pale blue skirt and her tanned legs peek at me from under the hem. Her white blouse hugs her curves in a way that I'd like to. She's beautiful. Angelic even. I've always thought so. Her beauty seems to shine through her stormy eyes, in her kind smile, and in the way she holds herself. Confident, poised, almost regal. There's a strength in this woman, but deep down, I have a feeling it's a cover for something she's hiding.

"Ryan, I—"

"Look Ki—"

She giggles as we both start at the same time. I gesture to the chair in the living area of my suite and she slowly slips into it. Her body is rigid and I wonder why she's scared. I can read her like a book and there's something on her mind. I hope she's not here to tell me she doesn't want me. Even after what happened yesterday, I want her. I love her dammit.

"Ryan, I needed to talk to you. There's so much about me that you don't know. That none of you know, but if you want to be with me then…" Her words taper off and I feel as if there's something I should do. Hold her. Or something. But I don't, I sit frozen as I watch the pain flit across her face, the agony dance in her pale blue gray eyes.

"Ki, there's nothing more I want than to be with you, but since you're with someone else, I just hope you're happy. That he's good to you." Edging forward on the sofa, I wait. Her eyes glisten with unshed tears and she nods.

"No! I am not with Josh. Then I need to tell you the truth. I didn't come here to see my ex-boyfriend as you thought. Or assumed after you saw me earlier. Yes, Josh was at my house to try to get me back, but he knows that will never happen. He saw me the first night I came home, I was having dinner with Dad and Josh was our waiter. Since then he's been calling the house, but I've refused to see him. He showed up unexpectedly. Of course, you decided to walk in at the same time he tried to force a kiss on me."

She sighs frustration evident on her face.

"The real reason I'm here is…" she stops, taking a deep breath before continuing. "I have had to get a few medical tests done." The words sink into me and my heart rate increases. The thud hammers at my ribs painfully and there's nothing I can do but wait for her to continue. "You see, I have the BRCA gene, my mother had it too. It's hereditary."

Her gaze is focused on the floor and I find myself on my knees at her feet. "Ki—"

"I lost my mother to cancer, Ryan. She… I mean, there wasn't…" When she blinks this time salty trails of sadness make their way down her cheeks and I can't stop myself from reaching up and swiping them with the pads of my thumbs.

"Baby." My voice is a whisper, raspy and filled with need to make her better. To somehow take her pain and make it mine.

"Ryan, I may not be able to have kids." Her words are blurted out and I'm sure it's louder than she intended because the shock on her face is evident. Her small body trembles under my touch and all I want to do is keep her safe. Safe from the agony that's so clear on her beautiful face.

"Kierra, baby, did you really think I'd walk away from you when you told me?" I question her, my tone is incredulous, but I'm more hurt than angry. My heart is filled with her and if she thinks that something like that is going to change that then she's wrong. And I need to make her see that.

"I just… I mean… Look, I didn't know what to think. Somehow, I feel like I'll fail as a partner if I can't give you babies, I know we're nowhere near that, but what man would want half a woman." Her words fuel my anger and I push up pulling her along with me. Our bodies flush and she molds to me like she's always meant to fit there.

"If I ever, and I mean ever, hear you call yourself half a woman I'll whip your ass so hard, you'll not sit down for weeks. You're all woman, Kierra Thorne, you're my woman. I love you so goddamn much. I wish you could see what I see when I look at you." I lean in and whisper the words over her lips. She smells like apples, sweet and delicious. I grasp her wrist and pull her toward the bedroom.

"Ryan, what are you doing?" She giggles and the tension that was heavy in the air only moments ago eases. I stop in front of the full-length mirror and pull her in front of me. We fit. Every part of her, fits with every part of me.

"Look, Kiki, can you see that woman

in there?" I point at her in the reflection of us. She nods slowly. Her eyes fill once again with emotion. "That's the woman I love, inside and out." I reach for the hem of her blouse and pull it up. Her hands instinctively lift and once I rid her of the material I growl at the soft pink bra that cups her breasts. They're not big, a handful, but they're everything I'll ever want. I unzip her skirt and it slips from her narrow hips pooling at her feet. The panties match her bra and her tanned skin against the pale shade is incredibly tempting.

"Ryan." She whispers my name and I shake my head to silence her. I want her to look, to really see the woman that she is. Because when I look at her, I see perfection. Not everyone is perfect, we're all broken in some way, but that's why we have soul mates, they see our perfection in our imperfections.

I undo the clasp of her bra, sliding it off her shoulders letting it fall to the floor. Cupping her breasts, I tease and tweak her nipples softly. Just enough to have her gasp and moan. "So beautiful. So perfect.

All mine." I've never been one to want to lay claim on any woman, never wanted to, only her. I trail my hands down her body and hook my fingers in the waistband of her panties. Slowly pulling them down her smooth toned thighs.

I recall she told me she'd done ballet when she was younger and it shows, her body is incredible. Toned enough to be sexy, and soft enough to be a woman.

When she steps out of the panties, I chuck them to the side and rise. Her scent invades my senses and I'm hard. My cock aching to be inside her again. I've only ever been with her one time and to be honest, I knew from that moment I'd need more. I'll always need more of her.

My hands splay on her soft stomach and I trail one down, cupping her heated core. The small strip of hair leading to her pussy is like a pathway to heaven, and I'd gladly die to go there.

My other hand trails up to her taut nipple, twisting it between my fingers. When I stroke her warm entrance her legs open wider. "Good girl, I want you to watch me touch you. I want you to see how much of a woman you are not only to me, but because you're you. Strong, beautiful, independent. You need to see how exquisite you are when you fall apart from my touch, from the pleasure I'm giving you and I want you to know, that's what I'll always give you. Pleasure." I whisper the words on her neck sending shivers through her body.

# KIERRA

His fingers dip into my pussy and I'm tempted to drop my head in pleasure, but I don't. I do as he's asked and watch. The scene is erotic, but romantic and sweet at the same time. It's as if I'm about to explode, to detonate and kill us both in the aftermath and what a way to go. "Look at this perfect pussy, Kierra. You feel how my fingers fit inside you?" I nod because there are no words to what this man is making me feel. "Look at your breasts, see how beautiful they are. Really look at yourself." As he talks his fingers pump into me and the knot in my stomach tightens, the need and ache I've had for him for all this time is tugging and pulling at me. Showing me how much we belong together.

"Ryan, oh God…" My moans are languid and my body is like putty in his hands. All I need is the release he's promising; the orgasm he's taunting me with. My toes curl into the soft carpet and I grip his hips behind me as my own buck and roll against his hand.

"Mmm, my beautiful Kiki. Do you like fucking my fingers, baby?" Those filthy words in Ryan's low timber skyrockets my need. As he growls in my ear every nerve in my body comes alive. My aching clit is hard and throbbing, needing his touch.

"Yes, Ryan, fuck." My words are incoherent as his hand moves faster, his fingers fuck me deeper and when he crooks them against a spot inside me my body flies apart and I cry out. The image of me coming from his touch is incredible and I feel my orgasm rip through me. Shuddering in his tight hold, my body softens against him, molding to him as he keeps me upright.

"So beautiful, Kiki. And you know what?" He whispers in my ear, teasing the lobe with his lips. "You are mine. Okay? All woman and all fucking mine." Slowly he slips his fingers from my drenched core and lifts them to my lips. "Taste yourself." I obey his command and lick the slick arousal from his digits. It's sweet and tangy, but watching him in the mirror while I do it is the most erotic thing I've ever done.

He grips my hips and spins me around. Leaning in, he licks and sucks on my lips, our tongues dart around, teasing each other and I suck on his, earning myself a deep groan. When we finally break apart, dark pools pierce me, holding me hostage in their hypnotic pull.

"Ryan." I utter his name with desire and his lips quirk into that sexy smile I've come to know and love.

"All mine. I want to make love to you now." I nod and he once again plants a kiss on my lips. Slipping his hand in mine, he tugs me over to the bed and lays me down. His movements are gentle and sweet, and when he pushes his briefs down I gasp at his rock-hard cock. I've seen it before, I've felt it inside me, but somehow at this moment it's bigger and thicker than I remember.

"Please, Ryan, I want you inside me." I lift up on my elbows and watch as he crawls onto the bed. There's no need for condoms and I'm grateful. After our first time, I told him I'm on the pill, and I trust him with my life. I know everything about this beautiful man.

He hovers over my body and a small needy whimper falls from my lips when the crown of his cock nudges my sex. Instinctively, my hips buck, and he chuckles at me. "Don't rush, Kiki, soon I'll be inside you. He reaches between us and leisurely strokes my sex, then grips his cock and teases me again by rubbing the crown up and down my pussy.

"God, Ryan, please. Just fuck me already." The words tumble in an order from my mouth and he doesn't waste anytime impaling me on his length. My nails dig into his back, and as I scratch down the smooth skin, his growl is evidence that I drive him as crazy as he does me.

"You feel so good. So perfect around

me." His husky words whisper over my breasts as he takes one taut nipple into his mouth suckling it, nibbling the sensitive bud.

My legs wrap around his waist as he fills me, over and over again. My body accepts him. We fit together like a melody with lyrics. "I need you faster." My hands reach down, gripping his tight ass, pulling him tighter against me as my moans echo along with the sound of skin, and the scent of sex mingles with the air around us. Our own erotic symphony.

"You're. Mine. Every. Inch. Of. You." He spears me with every word. Jolts to my heart diminish every fear and I'm falling into the abyss along with him. I love him. I need him.

My body bows against his, and he drives deeper sending me soaring. "Yessss…" I hiss out the word and dig my nails into his shoulders as his body locks and I feel him shoot jet after jet of release inside me.

Soft murmurs rouse me and when I roll over, I find Ryan on the phone. His back is facing me and I over hear him talking and I realize it must be Liam. "Yes, she's sleeping. We'll be home when we can, there are things we need to sort out. She's mine, I'm never leaving her." The words fill my heart and my eyes tear up with emotion. With love and devotion to a man who knows the real me and still wants me.

He hangs up a moment later and I shut my eyes quickly before he discovers me eavesdropping. "I know you're awake, baby," he chuckles and I crack one eye, peeking up at him. Dark eyes regard me with amusement. "How much of that did you hear?" He questions, climbing back under the covers, circling my waist, he tugs me against him and I bask in his warmth.

"Only the part about you telling Liam I'm the love of your life and you're not leaving me," I murmur on a shy smile. My voice groggy from all the moaning and screaming I did last night. There's a delicious ache between my thighs and I can't help smiling at the memory of how many times we made love last night.

"Good, that's the most important part." He plants a soft kiss on my forehead and my eyes flutter and my belly tingles with the flutter of butterflies. Ryan has a way of consuming me, my every thought, and my body. There's no explanation for what he does to me besides turning me to mush.

Last night, he both devoured me and claimed me, in every way possible. We got to know each other in ways that would make me blush every time I'd recall them. As if he were playing an instrument, he used my body to elicit sounds from me I didn't know I could make.

When I took him in my mouth, I savored his taste. Sweet, salty, just Ryan. I wanted to please him as much as he'd pleased me, and from the look on his face, I accomplished my mission. The faint hint of sunlight bathes us as we lie in each other's arms and I wonder if this is finally my happy ending.

Later today I'll see the doctor, get the results back from my blood tests. I've been religious about my health since I found out about the gene that's in my body, the one that could change my life forever, and already has. It's difficult as a woman to know your life is threatened by something so small, yet so volatile. I watched my mom suffer. I saw her deteriorate before my very eyes. A strong-willed, beautiful woman, weakened by a mutation in her body. When they found the cancer it was too far gone to treat. We didn't have a choice but to allow her to fade.

Months I spent by her side, but it wasn't only her, I watched my father disappear further into despair as he watched the woman he loved die. For years after she died, he retreated from himself, from me. Even though he did his best, it was something that I saw pained him. His heart was broken, fragmented with memories of her. Of their life together.

That's the reason I pushed Ryan away for so long. I didn't want him to go through that. I love him too much to know he'll be in such agony if he ever lost me. Or had to watch me go through that. "Ki?" His voice drags me from the millions of questions and thoughts running rampant through my mind.

Lifting my gaze, I meet his concerned stare.

"Are you okay, baby?" Nodding, I shift so I'm practically lying on his chest. Our faces inches apart and my mouth hungry to feel his lips on mine.

"I'm thinking, wondering how I got this lucky," I murmur.

"It's me that's the lucky one, Kierra. I don't want you worrying about anything. I'm here, I'm not leaving, and once your father gives me permission, I'm marrying you." His words, his confession stills my heart. Our eyes lock in a stand-off and as much as I want to deny him, to tell him to find someone who isn't threatened with an uncertain future, I don't. Instead, I smile. A real, genuine grin.

"I haven't agreed, and who knows, I may find some rich, sexy rock star who isn't as stubborn as you," I giggle when he tugs me closer.

"Don't even think about it," he mumbles into my hair. "Get some rest, and I'll go to the doctor with you later," he promises and as a yawn falls from my lips, I do fall under allowing myself to dream.

# RYAN

When I open my eyes all I see is her beautiful face. Angelic. Dark hair fans across the pillows and her full lips part as she breathes quietly. "Are you being a creeper?" Steel blue eyes open and peer at me.

"You're beautiful when you're asleep. I can't help but be creepy and watch you." I reach for her, pulling her into my arms. Her smooth skin is warm to the touch and her breasts are squashed against my bare chest.

"I guess since it's you, I'll be able to handle it," she quips in response and I roll us over, my body caging her in and I settle between her slender thighs. Our bodies align perfectly and my erection nudges her glistening pussy. The heat and slickness that meets the crown of my cock has me groaning with need and desire. Even though we spent most of last night making love, into the early hours of the morning, I want her again.

"Oh really?" I reach down and tickle her sides, which in turn has her giggling uncontrollably. She tries and fails to swat me away, I'm too strong for her and I've got her pinned to the bed.

"Please, please, stop. Okay, okay! I'm joking. Ryan!" Her giggles are like fuel to my blood, heating it with want. My body aches to be inside her. To feel her tight heat around me. Her wide eyes peer up at me and she murmurs. "Make love to me?"

"Sweetheart, you don't have to ask me twice," I growl. She's already drenched and I roll my hips, not sliding into her, just teasing her with the steel that is my cock. She's got me so hard, ready to make her scream my name over and over again.

I reach between us, stroking her pussy, then aligning my cock perfectly, I inch in slowly. Her body accepts me, like she's been made just for me. "You feel incredible, Kiki. You fit me like a glove." Her legs wrap around me and we move together in a beautifully erotic dance. Our hearts beat in time with the other. A rhythmic, calming melody that has my senses heightened, every nerve in my body is alight, sparking through me like a current of electricity.

This is our song. Between the want I have for her, and the fear she holds in her heart, I know we'll make this work. I've given up denying myself this woman. I'll have her, and it won't be for one night, or two, it will be forever. Until my dying breath. She just needs to let go, to finally relent and allow me to show her I'm man enough for her.

And with that thought running through my mind, we make love again. Uniting not only our bodies, but our hearts and souls. We're one. Always will be.

After breakfast, we both took a long, hot shower and Ki told me her doctor's appointment was at midday. Once we got dressed, I grabbed my keys, phone, and wallet and we made our way out to the reception to collect her car keys.

The road to her parent's house is quiet and my mind is whirling with thoughts of what her father's going to say. I wanted to ask for his blessing, but I didn't realize how nervous I'd be. I've never had a close relationship with my parents, but I know Kierra loves her father and his opinion counts. I've never been one to change who I am for others, if you don't like me, that's up to you, so this is out of my league completely.

I know if I had a daughter and a man like me walked up to the door asking for her hand in marriage, I'd lose my mind. I'd probably lock her up in a room and never allow her out. All I can do is hope he sees how much I love her. How much she means to me and that I'd never hurt her.

When we pull up to the house, I turn to her. She's tense and I wonder if it's because I'm with her, or because she knows what I'm about to do. "You're quiet," I comment, watching her reaction.

"I'm nervous, to be honest. My father

liked you when you first met him, that won't change now that we're officially together. It's just… well, today is going to be emotional in more ways than one and I really want him to see how I feel about you," her confession has my heart soaring. Hope blooms in my chest because she feels the same.

"I know, Ki, but even if he tests me, I'm not giving up. I love you. Do you understand that? I'm never walking away. If it takes me another ten years to prove to him how deep my feelings are, I'll do it gladly. If it will mean a forever with you, I'll move mountains, baby," leaning in, I plant a chaste kiss on her lips and sit back. The soft rosy hue on her cheeks makes me grin like a fool.

"I love you too, Ryan." She says so quietly, but I hear it. I've always heard her. Even when she wasn't saying anything at all.

"Let's go," I push the door open and exit the car. Rounding it, I open her door and offer my hand, as soon as hers slips into mine, I feel the confidence I need to get through this.

Before we reach the house, the door opens and I'm face to face with Mr. Thorne, Ki's father, and the man I need to convince to allow me to marry his daughter.

"Nice to see you again, Ryan," he rumbles in a deep baritone.

"Thank you, Sir. It's good to see you too. You're looking well," I reach out with a proffered hand and he accepts, allowing me to breathe.

"Come in, I've just made brunch," he turns and leaves us staring at each other. Giggling, Ki steps inside first and I follow, closing the door behind me. Their home is beautiful, filled with comfortable furniture with a lived-in feel. It's not a house, it's a home.

The living room opens onto a large dining table which overlooks a garden and swimming pool. There's a spread of food set out and even though we'd eaten a mere hour ago, I feel another bout of hunger kick in. It might just be nerves, but I settle in one of the chairs, with Kierra between her father and myself.

"So, Ryan," he starts and I drag my gaze to meet his. "You've come all this way to see my daughter? That's quite a trip." He doesn't sound angry, but there's definitely a wariness that filters through his words and hangs in the air.

"Yes, I..." Sighing, I take a sip of juice and regard him again. Better get this over with. "You see, Mr. Thorne, Kierra is special to me. I mean, I've known her for ten years. We've worked together, travelled the world together, and I've loved her for all that time. When I first saw her, my world stopped, it was as if she'd been put before me and I couldn't see anything else, or anyone else for that matter. I love her. I really do. And that's why I've come all this way," casting a quick glance at Ki, she offers a smile and I find the words, "I'd like your permission, your approval, your blessing to take her as my wife. I'd like to marry her, give her the support she needs in a partner, and I swear I'd never hurt her. I'll always be there for her, no matter what happens."

He's silent for a long while, too long and

my nerves get the better of me. He glances around, looks at his daughter and meets her gaze. Something passes between them, like an unsaid understanding and he pushes his chair out, rising to full height.

If I wasn't trying to swallow past the fear and anxiety lumped in my throat, I'd say more, but I can't. My voice has found a hiding place and I can't find it.

"Dad," Ki starts, but he glances at her, silencing her immediately. Then his gaze locks on me and Kierra's hand finds mine under the table.

"Ryan, thank you for coming here and being honest with me. For telling me about your feelings for my daughter, and also for caring for her when she's in L.A. Nothing would make me happier than her finding real love and a man who can offer her that. There's only one thing I need to know before I give you my blessing, and I will, but," he stops, so does my heart. He reaches for a magazine behind him and places it in front of both Kierra and me. When my gaze hits the headline, my heart lurches. My world crashes around me, dragging me down, deep into the darkness that I thought I'd escaped. The one thing from my past that I regret stares at me. Being a rock star has its perks, but it's also a curse. One that can ruin your life, your love, and your future.

"Ryan?" Kierra's voice breaks through the haze of fury and anger.

"Care to explain this accusation?" Her father's voice finally pulls my head up and I regard him. Honesty is the best policy, so I inhale a deep resounding breath and I know there's no other way out, but to give him the whole story.

# KIERRA

"I've made many mistakes over the years when it comes to certain choices I made. I have been with groupies, fans, whatever you want to call them, but I just don't remember this girl at all. Most of the time I was acting out of pure jealousy when I would see Kierra with her boyfriend at the time. I knew I wasn't man enough to admit my feelings, yet, the thought of not being with her set me off course. I did something stupid. Jealousy had wrung me out. I didn't know it at the time, but my love for her was already deep rooted."

He stops, glancing at me momentarily, then meeting my father's glare. I know what he's talking about because I recall that night with clarity. The band had finished playing and I'd been seeing Cody for a short while. We'd not slept together, but he was getting antsy with me. We were backstage when Ryan and the boys got off stage. That was when I did something I knew I shouldn't have. I pulled Cody in for a kiss that if it had been Ryan, would've made my toes curl and my belly flop, but I didn't feel a thing. I wanted to make Ryan jealous.

You see, as much as I refused to date him, I wanted him to want me. Yes, I was a bitch. I wanted him to feel the jealousy I felt when the groupies would grab him and kiss him. I needed him to experience the ache I felt seeing him with another woman.

"In my haze of frustration from seeing her kiss him, I did something I'd regret forever." His confession continues through my memories as I remember the girl on the front page of the tabloid sitting on the table, taunting me. "I got drunk, very drunk. It was the only way I would have gone through with it. You see, every time I kissed another girl, it was always gray-blue eyes that pierced me. It was always Kierra's face

I saw. Anyway, in my drunken haze I must have had sex with this girl. It's the only way to explain why I don't remember her." He glances at the offending pages before us.

My heart hurts at his confession. It's a physical ache.

"So you're telling me this was a one-night stand?" Hearing my father say something like that makes me cringe. You never think about your parents knowing about sex, one-night stands, or anything of the sort. It's something no child wants to think about.

"Yes, Sir. The first thing I'll have to request are paternity tests. It's been almost two years and I honestly don't know why she's surfacing now. The thing of it is, I don't remember that night. At all. Every time I try to figure it out, I come up blank. It's as if what happened has been wiped from my mind. Yes, she's claiming it's my child, but there's no proof. For someone in this business, proof is something that's called for, it's imperative we have tests done."

"This could be a lie she's fabricated to get you to pay her?" Ryan nods. His hand in mine feels warm and I give it a reassuring squeeze.

"I think she's lying, Dad. I know Ryan and as much as he's done stupid things, I don't think this is true, at all."

"Mr. Thorne, I know this might seem like too much for Kierra, and I agree it is. But, I love Kierra with all that I am. I don't want to hurt her, or pull her into this. I'm standing by her side no matter what. I'll show the world how much I love your daughter. There's nothing I wouldn't do for her."

My dad and Ryan are in a standoff, and as much as I love both men in this room, they're both stubborn. Deep down, my heart hurts for what this woman is doing to the man I love, but I know I need to guard myself. The news had to have broken early this morning, or last night when we were lost in each other.

As much as last night was perfect, doubt is a bitch and she loves to play with me. Since I was a teen, I'd worry. Things would always bother me, and this time, it's no different.

Yes, we've loved each other for a long

time, but what if it is his child. What if she's right and the little girl is Ryan's?

# RYAN

"Ryan, maybe you need to go back? To figure out what this woman wants?" Ki's sweet voice questions me, but I can't. There's no way I'm leaving her. Shaking my head, I rise from the table with a nod at Mr. Thorne and I step over to the terrace door.

"I'll leave you two to talk this out. Ryan," I turn to Kierra's father, "you seem like a good man, if my daughter believes in you, then I do too." With that, he turns and leaves us in the living room.

I turn to my girl. Taking her hands in mine, I hold them, feeling the heat of her smooth skin. "I'm not leaving you. This shit with her can wait. You're my life Kierra, don't push me away please?" She watches me with those stormy eyes.

"Ryan, I'll be okay. I have my dad. He'll be with me and when I get back, we can talk."

"Talk? What do you mean? There is no talking Ki, you're mine. This isn't a discussion. I'm with you. Always. It's been ten years and this time, I have you in my arms. I'm not letting you go."

The tension between us makes fear grip my chest. Breathing becomes difficult, and for the first time since I told her I love her, I feel as if she's slipping away.

"I want you to go, Ryan. This doesn't just affect you. It's the band. You've got to think about Callum and Liam as well." She nods then. "We can go to the hospital together. But after, I want you to go to them. To sort this out before it gets worse. It's a PR nightmare and with the tour coming up we need to put a lid on it."

"Always thinking about work, but if I need to make a statement, it will be here, beside you. Even with everything you've got going on, you're more concerned with us than yourself," cupping her face in my hands,

I lean in and press a kiss to her mouth. The sweetness of Kierra, is something I'd never tire of. My beauty. My muse. My inspiration.

Her soft moan is swallowed by the kiss as our tongues twist in an erotic dance. Her body curls into mine, fitting like a puzzle piece. Creating an incredible melody as we were meant to.

Finally, when I break the kiss, I meet beautiful gray eyes that swirl with too many emotions. "I love you, Ryan."

"And I love you, I always will." Nodding, she smiles then. One of her breathtaking smiles. A sight that will always still my heart.

"I better get ready, we need to leave in thirty minutes if we're going to make it on time to see the doctor."

"I'll be here." With a sweet smile, she turns and leaves me in the living room with my thoughts. I'm not leaving her again. Once she's been to see the doctor, we'll figure out what happens from there. I'll prove to her and her father that I'm the man that should be by her side forever.

"Ryan." A deep rumble of her father's

tone comes from behind me. When I rise, I find the man with the eyes that match my girls'.

"Mr. Thorne, I'm sorry about everything."

"There's no need to apologize. I've been in this world long enough to know when you're young and impressionable you can make the stupidest choices. I'm no different. However," he smiles then, settling in the armchair that faces a large screen TV. "When I met Clarissa, Kierra's mother, I knew what my heart wanted. There wasn't a doubt in my mind she would be my wife."

He chuckles. A faraway look in his eyes tells me he's remembering her. Kierra's mother.

"She was so beautiful. Exactly like Kiki. With the same feisty personality. All the years we spent together were the happiest I've ever been. Of course, when she got sick, I was beside myself. Nothing can ever prepare you for losing someone you love."

It's then that he meets my gaze dead on. His expression is serious, yet, his eyes tell another story.

"I can see how you look at her. I see the love between the two of you. Just remember, whatever the prognosis, she'll need a strong man, Ryan." His words are earnest, and I nod. She will need a strong man and that man will be me.

"I understand. I'm willing to do anything for her. Nothing she tells me is going to make me leave, unless she comes right out and tells me she doesn't want me. And even then, I won't give up on her."

The honesty lies in my words. The truth is in my eyes, and when he nods, offering me his hand, I gratefully accept it.

"What did my dad say to you?" She questions as we head to the private car I've arranged to drive us around. I don't respond until we're both seated in the back and she's informed the driver about where we're going. Taking her hand in mine, I plant a soft kiss on her knuckles.

I know I need to answer her, but all she gets from me is one word. "Nothing." I can feel her eyes on me for a moment before she turns her attention to the window.

"Ryan, I'm not stupid."

Chuckling, I reach for her thigh, placing my hand on it gently. "I never said you were. We spoke about what the future holds. There's nothing you need to worry yourself with, baby. It's fine. He shook my hand and we now have an understanding."

"So you both decided on my life without me in the room?" Her tone is filled with incredulity. That's one thing about my girl. She's a fireball. Independent, yet needing so much support and love. And that's the only thing you can give Kierra Thorne. There's no person that she'll cross paths with that won't come to love her in some way.

# KIERRA

"Yes, stop being so stubborn and let us care for you. Is it wrong of me and your dad to worry about you?" He murmurs quietly, his voice low and serious.

He's right. I can't stop them worrying about me, but I can stop them from making decisions for me. "I want to go home when this is over. We should take the private plane back to LA and try to sort out this PR nightmare. Tayla can't handle it alone."

"No, you're supposed to get treatment, if you need it. Once we have the go ahead from your doctor, then we'll talk about going home." His tone is adamant, but if there's one thing I've learned over the years, it's to never back down from what you want. Even though I pushed Ryan away, avoiding a relationship with him, when it was the only thing I wanted, I had my reasons. It seems now however, those reasons were moot. The man wants me and I want him.

"If I need any treatment I'll get it in LA with the doctor that's been monitoring me while I've lived there. The only reason I came back here was to see my doctor who did the procedure when I was nineteen and has my eggs stored away. He's the only one who knows my family history well enough to do the tests to see if it's safe to have a baby. He can give me the advice I need to make the choice."

"Okay, then you'll get the advice you need from him, get the tests done and I'll be right there beside you. It's time you stop pushing me away Kiki, I'm not going anywhere."

Sighing, I can't help loving this man. "So you're going to throw me over your shoulder and carry me back to LA caveman style?" I question on a giggle.

"If that's what it takes, then yes." There's no doubt in my mind that Ryan will do just that. If there's one thing I learned about Ryan over the past decade, it's that he doesn't take no for an answer. With the amount of times I've pushed him away, he's never given up.

As soon as we pull up to the hospital, dread fills me. It's been a long time coming and now as I sit here knowing I'm about to find out if I'll be able to have kids I can't stop my heart racing.

"Look at me," Ryan's tone pulls me out of the darkness I want to hide away in. Turning my attention to him, I meet his dark eyes. "We will get through this." His voice is filled with promise. With a vow to be by my side.

"Thank you, Ryan."

"No need to thank me. I just wish you'd told me sooner what was going on with you. You've pushed me away for long enough. No more. I'm not going to stand for it."

Once again, he's right. I haven't been able to let him in for so long, I can't understand how he just wouldn't relent. Most men would have given up. Not Ryan.

Smiling, I nod. "Yes, Mr. Callahan. You're

stuck with me now." He chuckles, nodding as he lifts my hand, planting a soft kiss on my wrist.

"Now, let's go in there and face this."

I inhale a deep breath as we exit the car and make our way, hand in hand, to the office of Dr. Horton. The man who was there for my mother through her treatments, and who then later spoke to me, giving me advice about my options.

As we walk into the reception area, we're met by one of the nurses. "Hello, how can I help you?"

"I've got an appointment with Dr. Horton at midday." She nods, rounding the desk, she settles in the chair and taps away at the computer.

"Kierra Thorne?"

"Yes." With a smile, she nods again, taps at the keys again and then she's rising to her feet.

"Come with me." I thought there'd be a waiting time, but it seems I'm ready to go to the slaughter. Shuddering, I glance at Ryan whose hand is holding onto mine tightly.

The long white hallway is stark. I've always hated hospitals. Even before my mum got sick, it was a place that filled me with dread.

"Here you are." The nurse pushes open a door, as we step inside I'm met with the sterile smell of medicine and cleaning products. "He'll be with you in a moment."

With that, we're left alone. The room itself has a desk, a large cabinet with glass shielded the boxes of medicines. The examination bed is in the far right corner with two chests of drawers with what I'm guessing to be medical equipment—needles, tubes, and whatever else I'd rather not think about.

"Hello Kierra." The doctor's deep voice comes from behind me as the door opens. He's dressed in the standard white coat. His graying hair is the only indication of how much older he is since the last time I saw him. The thin rimmed glasses perched on his nose are modern, but he peeks at me from above them.

"Hello, Doctor. It's good to see you again.

This is Ryan Callahan, my boyfriend." The words are foreign on my lips, but the smile that I get from the man I love is like a light in the dark.

"And you as well. Hello, I'm Dr. Horton." He offers Ryan a smile and they shake hands, but the hand on my shoulder never strays as the man I love offers all the support I need in one simple touch. "I'll need to see Kierra alone, there are a few tests I want to perform. You're welcome to sit outside and wait. She won't be long." The older man offers with a smile, but the way Ryan's hand squeezes my shoulder tells me he isn't happy with being sent outside.

"It's okay," I turn to face him. Assuring him that I'm in safe hands. I've known Dr. Horton since I was a child, so there's no need for him to worry. Endless brown orbs meet my steel gray ones. He's at war with himself, wanting to stay, yet knowing it will be okay if he doesn't.

He leans in after a moment, placing a soft kiss on my forehead. "I'll be outside." With that he turns to leave. Ryan's been the joker of the group, the one who always makes everyone else laugh, but when he shows his serious side it stills my heart. He's a rock, a boulder in my life holding down everything threatening to blow away.

"Looks like a good man." I turn to face the doctor with a smile and nod.

"He is." My affirmation earns me a satisfied grin. "What do I have to do first?"

"Blood and saliva samples and I'll have to send those off for testing. I don't want you to worry, Kierra. We'll figure this out." Nodding, I inhale a deep breath and hope he's right.

# RYAN

My mind is running riot. The doctor asked me to wait outside while he examined Ki, and took the blood samples. It's only been twenty minutes, but it feels as if it's been an hour, possibly more.

Running a hand through my unruly hair, I push off the chair and head toward the coffee machine near the entrance. Once I have a cup in hand, I settle back down outside the room where my girl is.

Nothing could ever prepare you for something like this. Learning that the person you love may be ill, or may one day no longer be around. We all know life is short, it's a fragile existence and so many lose those they love without telling them how they really feel.

I take a long gulp of my coffee, savoring the bitter taste. Just then, the door opens and Kierra appears. "I'm done, he's going to get the last test results and we'll be able to get an idea on the time frame. All the previous scans look good. He's positive I can do this. My ovulation time is coming up, so… Well I might be able to get the procedure done."

Nodding, I immediately rise and go to her, pulling her into my arms. "Anything you want. Are you okay?" She nods, but her body is cocooned in the crook of my arm. Every time I hold her I'm in awe of how perfectly she fits in my arms.

As we head out of the building and into the sunlight, she unravels herself from my hold and glances at me. "Thank you." Her words are soft, whispered, but I hear them.

"I told you, I'm here for everything. All the ugly and all the beautiful moments." When we reach the car, I open the door and allow her to slip into the bench seat. I round the car and settle in beside her. "Back to the hotel," I inform our driver and he nods. Turning to my girl, I question. "So, what did he say?" The engine starts and we head out of the parking lot and onto the street.

"Basically they'll test my blood and saliva to determine how dormant the gene is. If they think it's safe, I may have a chance at implanting the eggs. However," she murmurs, then stops.

Casting a quick glance at her, I notice she's biting on her lower lip. "What, Ki?"

"He said if I do want children… I mean… If I decided to take a chance, I would need… I…" Her mumbling has my body alert and my hands gripping the wheel in a white knuckle hold.

"Just tell me, baby. You're not going to scare me off."

"He is concerned about me carrying to full term, although it's possible, he did mention that I would need to be very careful." She casts her stormy eyes at me, then a small smile appears on her face. "If I do decide to go through with the procedure, it will be done via IVF."

Nodding, I flit my gaze to her, taking in the worry etched on her face. "You know I'll be there with you no matter what happens. And if this is something you want, I will do it for you. IVF doesn't scare me, baby. If that's what it takes, then we'll do it," I offer confidently.

"You're an amazing man, Ryan Callahan. I mean, this is something I've just sprung on you and you're still here. Most men would have run a mile."

"Kiki, there's nothing I'd rather do, and I thought you knew by now, I'm not most men," I retort cockily which earns me a swat on the arm. "But all jokes aside, this is us. You're going to have my baby, whether we do it the natural way, or the medical way." Reaching for her hand, I give it a reassuring squeeze as I pull into the parking lot of the hotel. "And I think now is the perfect time to show you just what I mean."

"Ryan—"

"Let's go, we'll have a late lunch, relax in the suite and talk." Exiting the car before she can respond, I'm at the passenger side before she can move. I offer her my hand, and when she slips hers into mine, I revel in her warm touch.

The trip to the door of my suite is silent. I know she has a lot on her mind, but I want her to try to stay calm. Things will work out. I know it. I've never been an optimist, but with her, I feel as if I can allow myself to believe in happiness, in things working out.

I unlock the door with the keycard, allowing her to enter first. "I forgot how beautiful these rooms were," she murmurs, stepping up to the window which overlooks the city. It's one of the smaller suites, but it's still remarkably large with a living area and separate bedroom.

Stepping up behind her, I wrap my arms around her waist. My chin rests on her shoulder as we both take in the view below. "All those people down there. They're all going through something, life isn't easy. It's fucking difficult, there are trials and tribulations in everyone's journey, but you," I spin her around, so her steel blue eyes are on my dark brown ones. "You're not alone. Besides the family you have back in LA, you have your dad who loves you more than anything. And even besides him, you have me. As much as I wanted to do this a different way, I think it is the perfect time."

"What do you mean?" Her brows furrow in confusion, I respond with a smirk. I knew there'd be the perfect time and place to do this. I thought it would be on stage, but with Ki and I, we've never been one for the spotlight, and this right here is our time.

Dropping to my knee, I tug the small box I've had with me since the day we returned from Callum's wedding. I bought it that very day and I knew the perfect opportunity would present itself. "Kierra Thorne, it's been too long. I've waited, I've plotted," I chuckle, meeting her pretty eyes which are now glistening with unshed tears. "But now it's time I claimed my woman. That may sound like a caveman, but with you, I am. I'm selfish because I want to be the only one who makes you smile. I'm greedy because all I want is to spend every moment with you, and I'm so in love with you, I can't see myself with anyone else."

When she blinks, the steady flow of tears

streams down her cheeks. She's incredibly beautiful. The small smile on her face tells me I'm not making a fool of myself, but deep down, I'm scared she'll push me away again.

"So, after all that rambling, I want you, here and now, to say yes to being my wife. To having a family with me, whether it's our biological child, or if we have to adopt, or even look at a surrogate. To making me happy for the rest of my life, just by gifting me your smile. Through whatever trials and tribulations, we have to face, know that you'll never be alone."

Releasing her hand, I snap open the small velvet box, and offer her the single diamond ring. She's quiet and my heart stutters against my chest. "Yes." The one word she finally utters sounds around me like a siren. I leap up, pulling her into a tight hug, needing her body against mine. Feeling her heart beat at the same rhythm and her scent filling my senses.

When we finally break apart, I plant a gentle kiss on her lips and tug the ring from the cushion, slipping it onto her finger. I guess Liam was right, I'm taking her back to LA with a shiny diamond on her ring finger, but I'll definitely not tell him he was right.

"I love you, Ryan." Her voice is laced with heavy emotion and I meet her stare.

"I love you too, Kiki."

# KIERRA

Never did I think that when I got on that plane I would have Ryan follow me all the way across the world and proposing, but if I've learned one thing about this man, it's to expect the unexpected. "Let's get you fed, soon-to-be Mrs. Callahan." Ryan's mouth lifts into a satisfied grin and I can't help giggling. I take him in, every part of him is perfect to my eyes. The dark scruff on his chin covers a sharp jaw line, deep brown eyes that remind me of melted chocolate, and full lips that curl into a satisfied smirk every time he looks my way.

"I like the sound of that." My response is confident as the thought of being Mrs. Callahan sends my stomach into a flurry of tingles. I lean up onto my tip toes and plant a kiss on his lips.

"Room service? Unless you wanted to go down to the restaurant in the hotel?" Knowing if we went outside we'd probably be bombarded by fan girls, I shake my head. I want time alone with him. To revel in the happiness that's now surrounding me.

"Let's stay in, I'll call my dad and let him know what the doctor said. I'm sure he's worried about me." With that, we set about with Ryan calling room service, and me calling my dad.

Once I've finished my call, I head out onto the balcony. The evening is warm, with a slight breeze billowing my brown wavy hair. "All sorted?" Ryan's deep timber comes from behind me and I nod.

"Yeah, he's going to meet with some friends, it's bowling night." I tell him as he encircles me in his arms. "Did you order dinner?"

"I did. And I've asked them to bring some dessert too." He murmurs in my ear, his lips whispering over the shell, which sends a shudder through me.

"Behave."

"I am. I was just thinking of having a starter," his rough growl has goose bumps erupting on my arms. He leans in further, suckling the sensitive skin on the nape of my neck. "Mm, delicious," he mumbles, earning himself a giggle.

"Stop, we're going to get our dinner soon and then you can feast on me," I retort playfully.

"You better remember that, little lady." Finally, he steps back, allowing me to cool myself down from the heat of having his mouth on me, his hands gripping me, and his toned, chiseled torso against me. As much as I want to be with him, I'm still nervous. I'm not sure why.

Just then, there's a knock at the door. "Dinner's here." He announces as he makes his way through to open for room service. The sound of the trolley sounds through to the living area. Upon entering, I take in the amount of silver dishes.

"There's enough here for an army. Are you crazy?" I gasp in surprise. There's definitely enough to feed a small country.

"I didn't know what you wanted, so I got a little bit of everything." He shrugs nonchalantly. Lifting the lids of two platters, he reveals one with cheese and meat, and the other is filled with fruit. "There's also lasagna, and I've asked them to bring a salad, I think it's Greek."

"Ryan, this is too much."

His dark gaze falls on me then. "Nothing's ever too much for you, sweetheart." Who said romantic men don't exist, because the one I've found, has it in spades.

"That was incredible." I feel like I'm about to explode. We've pretty much attacked everything they've brought except for a small bowl which Ryan has forbid me to open. There's not much of anything left and I have to lean back against the sofa to take a breather.

"I told you we'd make a dent in the pile of food," he chuckles beside me, leaning over, he kisses me lightly on the cheek and rises from the sofa. I watch the way his jeans hug his ass and thighs when as he walks to the trolley, setting the plate down. "Wine?" Trailing my eyes up to his face, I find him cockily smirking at me. "Enjoying the view, baby?"

"Always," I quip. He turns to regard me fully.

"I think it's time we had dessert," he growls suddenly. The rough timber of his tone, the lust lacing his words send a jolt of need zipping down my spine and desire tingles between my legs.

"And what did you have in mind, Mr. Callahan?"

In three long strides, he's before me, both hands proffered. "Up," he orders, I obey. Slipping my hands into his, he tugs me up. Our bodies flush, with heat swirling around us. He takes one step back and watches me with those dark eyes. "I want to watch you strip," he says, a hint of a smile on his suddenly serious face.

"Ryan—"

"Kierra, I'd like to watch you slowly strip out of that dress, then I want to watch you unclasp your bra allowing it to pool at my feet. Then, I'd like you to turn around so I can see that pretty ass while you slip your panties over your hips, down those long legs and have you taunt the fuck out of me while you offer me glimpses of your sweet pussy. Do you think you can do that?"

He settles himself in the armchair a few feet away from me, tugging off the gray T-shirt he was wearing, he affords me with a view of his chest. The light dusting of hair that adorns his well-toned pectorals lead down to well defined abs and those V muscles pointing to the hidden thickness behind his zipper. Just below his belly button is a fine strip of dark hair, a trail to something I'm aching to feel fill me.

Slowly, I reach for the hem of my dress, tugging it up to my hips. The silence is deafening as he leans back, his one hand on the crotch of his jeans. His gaze burns into me as I lift the material up and over my head. My skin is on fire merely from his gaze.

"You're perfect, baby," he murmurs reverently. With such passion it knocks the breaths from my lungs. "Look at me, Kierra." Once again, he orders, his tone low, calm, yet demanding at the same time. When my eyes meet his, I'm locked in the searing desire that's so evident in them. "You're beautiful."

He lifts his hand for me to continue, so I do. Unclasping my bra as he asked, I allow it to fall at his feet. My hands are trembling as I turn and allow him a view of my ass in the tight blue cotton material.

"Fuck."

It's a grunt, a growl. Hooking my fingers in the waistband, I slowly tug them down. As soon as they pass the curve of my cheeks, I bend at the waist pushing them lower. A hiss from behind me has me smiling. Being able to taunt him like this has me turned on beyond imagination.

Once the flimsy material is on the floor, I step out of them. At the same time, I take off the sandals on my feet. I'm bare. Naked to his scrutiny. Turning around, I face him once more. "Is that what you had in mind, Mr.

Callahan?" I question, tipping my head to the side. His face is a picture. Desire dances in his eyes to the tune of my heartbeat. The thrumming between my legs spikes when he unzips his jeans, shoving them down thick thighs. His cock, thick and hard, has my mouth watering.

"Come here, baby. I want those pretty lips on my dick."

# RYAN

This woman has no idea how perfect she is. How beautiful, intoxicating. She kneels before me, her gaze darkens, pupils dilate as she watches me stroke my steel shaft. "Do you see what you do to me, Kiki?" I question, my voice raspy with need. She nods, her teeth chewing her lower lip in a sweet, innocent, yet naughty way.

Releasing my cock, I watch as she reaches for me. Her delicate hand wraps around me and my eyes roll back in my head. *Jesus fucking Christ.* With slow steady movements, she strokes me. Her fingers teasing the pre-cum on the tip.

Suddenly her warm mouth engulfs me sending me soaring. "Fuck, Kiki," I bite out, grinding my teeth together. She ignores me, cupping my balls as she takes me deeper. Pleasure shoots through me. As if I've just shot up, straight into the vein. I'm high. I'm addicted. I'm hers.

Her head bops up and down as she sucks me like she's been born to do it. A soft hum from deep in her throat zips through my shaft straight to my balls. I'm going to come if she doesn't stop.

"Baby, enough. Please," I beg. Pleading with her, but she doesn't relent. Her mouth continues to pleasure me like it's her last job before she leaves this earth. This woman will be the death of me. "Kierra," I grunt as she immediately allows me into her throat and I'm gone. My hips jerk as my orgasm sends me reeling.

Gripping the material of the sofa, I tug at it as I fuck her mouth shooting jets of my hot release into her throat. Every drop is swallowed by my goddess. Her movements slow as she lifts her head off me, licking me until I'm free of the heat of her mouth.

"Was that what you had in mind?" Her lips curl into a sinful smirk. Jesus, this woman.

"Naughty girl. Up, I want to return the favor." Tugging her up, I position her on the sofa, bent at the waist with those lithe legs spread open. Her smooth glistening pussy greets me as a soft needy moan escapes her lips. "Such a pretty pussy, baby." I whisper over her sensitive flesh. Reaching up, I grip both cheeks of her pert little ass and open her to my gaze.

With no more words between us, I flatten my tongue, lapping at the sweetness of her cunt. "Oh, God!" She cries out as my tongue darts into the slick folds of her core. She's wet, drenched. I feast on her body like it's my last meal. Like I need more of her to survive. To live. Because I do.

With one hand gripping her ass, I use the other to tease her. Slipping two fingers into her tight heat, I finger fuck my woman until she's squirming. Her whimpers, mewls, and soft sounds of pleasure have me harder than I've ever been. Her pussy is tight, pulsing around both digits I now have inside her. Dragging my fingers out, I circle her clit, taunting the hardened nub.

"Please, please, oh fuck," she moans, louder now. I know she's close. Her thighs tremble as I continue my pace. Unrelentingly fucking her with my fingers, needing the sweetness she's about to gift to me.

"Come for me, Kiki. I want to taste that delicious cunt of yours all over my face. I want those juices coating my tongue." I order her, my tone rough. My cock is solid again, needing to drive into her. To mark and claim her. To show her how beautiful she is with only our bodies.

Dipping both fingers back into her pussy, I use my thumb to tease her clit which sets her off. The orgasm rips through her, causing her to shudder. My mouth is on her in a second, lapping at her release. Fucking perfectly delicious.

Before she can recover from the aftershocks, I pull my fingers from her, rising, I slide into her. My cock fully seated in her tight body. "Fuck, Kierra, you're so tight." I grunt, gripping her hips as I pull out and slam back into her.

"Ryan, please… oh, Ryan… god… fuck…" Her voice is hoarse from crying out my name and I don't stop, I can't. Her body squeezes my cock, pulling me deeper into the heat of her pussy.

"That's my girl. You hear that?" I question. Her head moves, I think she's nodding, but her body is shuddering with another release which only serves to confirm she's mine. I own her body, every fucking orgasm is mine. "You're mine, Kierra."

My words are grunted through thrusts. Our skin slapping against each other in an erotic symphony mingle with the whimpers of the woman I love. Her grip on the sofa is white knuckle tight as I continue to fuck her. This is rough, passionate and it's everything I want to show and give her.

I'm hers. She's mine.

Reaching around her, I tweak her clit, tugging it causing her to cry out again, and again. My name. It's my fucking name. The thought sets me off and I slam into one last time, filling her with not only my cock, but jets and jets of hot seed.

When I finally still, I stroke her back, running a fingertip down her spine. "You're so beautiful." I mumble. Turning her head, she regards me with shimmering eyes. "Why are you crying?" I question, startled. My cock slips from her body and I immediately miss her heat.

"I love you." Three words she breaths as she strokes my face. Her touch jolting my heart. "I just love you." Again, she tells me the same words and I can't help smiling.

"And I love you," I vow. Reaching for her, I lift her, bridal style and walk her into the bathroom. "We need a shower."

"Now that sounds like fun," she giggles, stepping into the two-person shower and turning on the spray. When I join her, the water slowly warms and I pull her into my arms.

I grab the body wash and pour some into my hand. Rubbing them together, I massage her shoulders. "Thank you, baby," I say quietly. Enjoying the feel of her skin.

"For what?"

I'm not sure how to answer her. I can't

find the words to explain to this woman how much she's given me. Agreeing to be my wife, to allow me to be the man beside her as she goes through life, she's gifted me the family, I never thought I'd have. Besides Callum and Liam, Kierra is offering me something special. She's giving me her forever. It's a gift I will never tire of, but how do I tell her that.

"For being you."

# KIERRA

"Mum, tell me what's going on?" Her striking blue eyes are filled with tears. Something's not right. This feels all wrong. My chest restricts painfully in my chest making it difficult to breathe.

"Kierra, baby girl. I'm so sorry." Confusion settles in my mind, heavily weighing down on what I've just overheard.

"Sorry about what?"

"The doctor... I was going to tell you, but things have been so busy for you. You've been through too much. I... I'm scared you'll have to go through this one day, I had to get all the facts before I told you."

"You're not making sense, Mom. What are you talking about?"

She shakes her head sadly. My own tears blur

my vision and I take in the woman I've known all my life. Her strength is the only thing that got me through my teenage years. She's been my pillar, my rock. But seeing her so broken, so torn apart has my fears skyrocketing.

"I'm dying, Kiki. They've confirmed the cancer. It's spread too far. Stage four." The room spins. My head swirls. My vision blurs. I'm not sure who's screaming. I think it's me. It's a sob so loud, so filled with pain that it physically hurts. As if it's stabbing my chest.

A sharp blade. Her words are muffled. I can't hear anything. It feels as if my ears are blocked. There are arms around me. Strong arms. Pulling me into an embrace.

It should soothe me. It should calm me. But it doesn't.

There's that noise again. A screech drenched in agony.

Dying. Dying. Sick. Sick.

No. It can't be. She can't be. My mother. My rock. I can't.

"Kiki… Kiki…" My name. Someone's calling me but the pain is too much. My breathing is uneven, difficult. I can't.

"Kierra!" Jolting up, I find the affectionate gaze of Ryan. "Baby, look at me," he pleads and I do. Wrapping me in his arms, I settle with the lingering pain of the nightmare still so fresh in my mind. I lost her. She's never coming back. Tears burn my eyes. "You're safe. I'm right here, Ki." The deep tone of Ryan's voice is enough to calm the ache, the fear that overrides my mind.

"My mom… She's…" I'm not sure what I'm trying to say.

"Kierra." He cups my face, making me look at him. "You're not alone. Since the moment I saw you, I was yours. We lost our way a few times in between but I'm here for you. I'll always be here for you."

His promise is endearing. Honest and raw. After all the time we've been together, those times we've spent in the same house, this is something different.

I didn't want to believe it before. But there's no denying it now. He knows where I come from, why I kept him at an arms distance. The truth that now lies between us is more than I could ever ask.

"Ryan, I'm scared." For me to admit that takes a lot. Not because I'm proud, but because I think if I do admit it, perhaps my worst fears will come true. And the last thing I want is for that to happen.

"It's okay to be scared, baby. You can't be strong all the time. That's not how life works. And when you're scared, I'll be there to hold you and take those fears away. Don't ever hide how you feel from me." He implores me with those dark eyes that sear me. Burning down my walls and finding the scared girl beneath. The one who hid away when her mother died. The one who put on the fake smile and made her way across the world to live her dream. That's the girl I want to say goodbye to because I'm no longer her, I'm a grown woman.

Most of my adult life I spent afraid. Too scared to let anyone in. So, when I knew I'd fallen for Ryan, I pushed him away. I told him we were friends, nothing more because I couldn't see the day he walked out of my life. Now, as he sits here cradling me in his strong arms, promising me he's not going anywhere, for the first time in a very long time, I allow myself to believe. To cry. To expel all the fear, pain, and worry.

"I'm here, Kiki, if you need to cry then do it. Break down if you must, but know I'll always keep you safe. You're mine. Always." He promises again. I think he has it in his mind that if he tells me enough times I'll one day believe it, but he doesn't need to, because I do.

"I'm yours." I murmur. "As soon as I know what the results are, I'd like to go home. I was also thinking of asking my dad if he'd like to come with us." I tell him honestly. I've missed having Dad close by, spending time on long phone calls to him has been difficult because I never want to say goodbye, but if he's willing, I'm sure we'd be able to get him across the ocean. My Dad hated the last two flights he took to visit me. He always says people weren't meant to fly which makes me giggle.

"Then you should ask him. I'm sure he'd want to be close to you again. Do you think he would?" Ryan asks quietly, his lips on my cheek.

"He mentioned that he'd like to move, but with us needing to plan a wedding, and your new tour, I'd like to have him there. He'll love being close to the ocean, since he grew up in a seaside town. There's no doubt that he'll make friends. You've seen him when he visited." My response earns me a chuckle.

The memory of my dad and the way he'd just walk out onto the sidewalk and find someone to chat to makes me smile. He's always been like that. Everywhere we went, it was always my dad who'd come home with a contact, or connection for someone he'd just met. Whether they're travelers or just local contacts, he was the most outgoing of the two brothers. My uncle on the other hand, he was always a recluse. When he passed away, there were a handful of the people he'd known at his funeral, including family.

"Then we'll take him with us. If he's not ready to go yet, I'm sure Cal wouldn't mind getting Demitri to fly out." Nodding, I turn to face the man I love.

"Thank you for taking my fears and making them your own."

"I'll always do that, baby. I promise." And as he tells me that, I know it's true.

# RYAN

We've just arrived at Dr. Horton's office, the tension rolling off Ki is nothing short of turbulent. She's like a little thunder storm waiting to take out anything in her way. He called an hour ago asking her to come in to talk about the test results.

To say that I'm nervous would be an understatement. I want everything to work out, for Kierra to experience having her own child. And yes, I'm selfish because I want it to be our baby, biologically. "Hello to you both." A rumble comes from behind us as the doctor enters the room. He offers us both a smile as he settles on the large leather chair behind the wooden desk.

"Is there something wrong, Doctor?" Kierra's tone is filled with anxiety which spikes my worry. The graying man shakes his head, opens the file before him, then lifts his blue eyes.

"On the contrary, everything is just fine. With the results that came in, it looks like the gene is dormant in your body at the moment. This means if you want to go ahead with the in vitro procedure we can do it. I've also done a pre-implantation genetic diagnosis on the embryo's and there are no concerns there."

Silence falls around us, and when I turn to my girl, I notice the moisture on her cheeks. "Ki, babe." She turns to me then, her eyes a mixture of a cloudless sky and a silver with the shimmer of tears.

"I'll give you two a moment." Dr. Horton rises, closing the file, he makes his way out of the room. Once the click of the door sounds the tears stream down Kierra's face.

"I-I don't… I-I mean…"

"Baby, look at me," my order is soft, murmured in her ear. She lifts her head to regard me and I cup her face in my hands. "We'll do this okay. If it's what you want, then we will go through with the procedure."

"But—"

"Listen to me, Kierra Thorne. I want you, I want this, there's no buts, only yes or no. So, if you want to try this, if you feel like you're strong enough, then I'm right here." I tell her this without blinking, searching her gaze, imploring her with mine. Hoping she'll understand that this is the only thing I want and need. Her.

"I want to, Ryan. I want to try this. There's nothing I want more than to have my own baby, to carry to full term without the fear of he or she being sick, or even myself. I just—"

"Then we'll do it. Me and you, Kierra." I vow. Our gazes are locked. Our hands are intertwined and our hearts… Those beat together, creating the song that only our souls know.

"Okay, I'd like to do it here. Before we go back." There's still that annoying tabloid about Ryan possibly having a child with someone else which for some reason irks me. She's waited two years to suddenly appear with this little girl. I've emailed Tay a press release to confirm we'll be asking for a paternity test before making any further comment. If this *Tiffany* for one moment thinks she's getting my man, she's got another thing coming.

"We can. I'll need to make a statement about the paternity claim. I don't know why she's appeared suddenly wanting to stir shit up, but if this is where you want to do it then we'll stay. I'm not leaving you when you're having to do this."

"What if the child is yours?" Her question hangs in the air between us. Emotion swirls like a lead weight. Taking her hand in mine, I look into those deep blue eyes and make my promise.

"I'm not leaving. If the child happens to be mine, I'll take responsibility, but Kierra, I promise you, my heart, mind, body, is yours. Nobody will come between that."

She nods then. "Then you'll just have a little girl with another woman."

"I'm sorry this is happening, adding to the stress you're having to go through, but we'll have our own child together. It will work out, Kiki. We will make it work." She kisses me then, it's a soft, soul stealing kiss, and I bask in it. In her love.

"That's what we'll do," she murmurs against my lips.

Since we decided to take a chance and have her eggs fertilized almost a week ago, I've donated my sperm and they've fertilized the eggs. Dr. Horton said it takes two to six days for the growth to happen and Kierra will go in for the implantation.

I'm nervous, excited, and I'm anxious. Today we're going into the hospital where the woman I love is going to have the eggs transferred to her. The timing couldn't be more perfect apparently since Kierra's cycle is at the right time to have the procedure done. I can tell she's anxious to go home, back to LA, I'm not sure if it's nerves about what she's about to face, or if she's just needing an escape.

Me on the other hand, all I can think about is marrying her, wanting her to have my child. If this is the only chance she gets, I pray with all I am that the procedure works. I want to see her glow from the pregnancy. To see her body change as she carries a baby would make me the happiest man. Not only because she'll have my child, but because this will be her only chance for it.

Too much of her life has been governed to her by medical professionals. Just this once, I want her to be able to have what every woman should be able to have.

To experience it. To feel a baby, move inside her. The miracle. The beauty of it.

I wonder now if I'd told her sooner. Been honest with my feelings about how much I wanted her. So many times, over the years I almost did. Would it have made a difference? Would we still be here trying to have a baby the medical way? Yes. I know we would because I love her.

"Ryan, are you ready?" Her voice startles me out of my inner dialogue. She's dressed in a short pale blue dress with those silver strappy sandals. Her hair is loose in wet waves since she's just come out of the shower.

"I am. Are you?" I'm not sure if she can hear the tension in my tone, but it's there, heavy, unyielding. I want to be strong for her, to give her the support she needs, but deep down, I can't stop the fear from overriding every thought in my mind.

"I guess so. There's no turning back now. Not that I want to. I mean, I've wanted this for so long. And you... I mean... Are you nervous? Is it just me?" Her rambles are adorable, calming me instantly. She's got this way about her where she'll mumble about things that's on her mind, it's the reason I can't help smiling when she's around. That, and of course her beauty. This woman is like a blaze in the darkness. A lightning strike through the darkened sky.

"Babe," I murmur, rising from the sofa where I was perched. Stalking toward her, I grip her slim hips, tugging her against me. "If you don't stop rambling, I'm going to show you exactly what I want to do to that pretty mouth." Her breathing hitches at the elicit threat that turns the air around us into a sexually charged storm. "Everything is going to be okay."

"Okay. Okay. I believe you. Now stop making sexual innuendo's and let's go. We can't be late." Chuckling, I step back, releasing her from my hold. With my phone in hand, we head out of the suite. This is it. I'm about to become a father. The thought has me smiling from ear to ear.

# KIERRA

One week. Seven long days since they did the IVF procedure and it took. I'm sitting at the airport with a positive pregnancy test in my bag, a diamond ring on my finger, and Ryan beside me with the biggest smile on his face. We're finally heading home. Since Dad wanted to stay to finalize all his affairs, he said he'd follow us out later. I knew he'd want to spend time in the home he and Mom lived in for most of their married lives.

The long flight home will give me time to figure out what we're going to do once we land.

I haven't told Tay or Emm about the baby, neither have I told them about getting engaged. We've both decided it would be much better as a surprise. One hell of a fucking surprise, but one none the less. I can't wait to see the look on their faces when we walk into the house with all this news.

Excitement has my stomach fluttering. "You okay, Kiki?"

"Yeah, I'm just thinking about telling everyone about the pregnancy."

"It will definitely be a bomb drop, but I think it's been a long time coming. But I've loved you for as long as I can remember and the Hayes brothers know that."

"Yes, that they do. Even the girls know."

He reaches for me as the plane makes its way down the tarmac. "I want the world to know," he affirms with a smile. When those full lips land on mine, the plane takes off and I'm sure the flurry in my stomach is more from the kiss than from being airborne.

The flight was an easy one, thankfully and when we touch down, the buzz of excitement flits through me. I'm going to see my girls. Even though I grew up as an only child, I always wanted a brother or a sister and life has now afforded me with Tay and Emma, as well as Cal and Liam. Technically, I work with all of them, but we're more like a family than anything else.

"Ready to do this?" Ryan asks from beside me. His eyes a shining with the excitement I feel.

Nodding, I inhale a relaxing breath. "It's now or never." Disembarking the private plane, we head out toward the small hangar away from the paparazzi and journalists that I'm sure have heard about Ryan being out of the country.

Once we step inside the building, Emma comes bounding toward us. She pulls me into a warm sisterly hug, "I've missed you." She murmurs into my hair.

"And I've missed you, every one of you."

"Hey man." Comes Liam's tone from beside me. Before I have a moment to say anything, the cocky drummer grabs my left hand and starts chuckling. "What did I say?" He settles his gaze on Ryan who gifts him an eye roll. "Come here, little sis," he smirks, lifting me up and spinning me around.

"What are you two on about?" I question while being twirled by Liam.

"I'm not saying it." Comes the response from Ryan, yet Liam sets me down, not saying a word. The look on his face tells me the two of them either had a bet going, or something.

"I told him you'd be back here with a shiny diamond on that ring finger." The man I consider a brother tells me confidently and I can't help shaking my head.

"I'm so happy for you, love." Emma smiles, offering me a quick hug before grabbing my hand inspecting the ring. "It's beautiful."

"Thank you, he surprised me. It came out of the blue."

"Oh yeah right, like you didn't know the man had blue balls for you." The comment earns Liam a punch on the shoulder from Ryan.

"Shut it. Let's go." My man grunts in frustration. As we make our way toward the parking lot, I can't help smiling at where I am right now. Life has taken a turn and it's given me more than I could ever have asked for or imagined.

Once my dad arrives, my family will be complete. My heart aches for my mom, if only she were here to see me, I know she'd be happy for me. She'd be proud.

"Tay is going to go nuts, she's been busy, but Callum has been driving her crazy with his overprotectiveness. I think having you both back will hopefully ease that." Emma informs us as we get into Liam's BMW X5.

It's not far from the airport to the house and I'm anxious to finally tell them all the news. Especially about the baby.

"He's never going to ease up, you do realize this? My brother is a pain in the ass when it comes to his woman."

"And you're not?" Emma quips him playfully, to which Liam can only grunt. He is as bad as his brother, but Ryan's no better. He's been overly attentive since the procedure and even though I haven't experienced anything abnormal, and I've told him so, he's still concerned. Until we have the test results in a month or two when we can finally see the baby, hear the heartbeat, get the all clear, I know he's going to treat me like a fragile doll.

Once we reach Cal and Tay's house, Liam kills the engine and we all exit the car. Ryan grabs our bags from the trunk and we head toward the house. Before we make it to the door, Callum and Tayla meet us outside, and we're once again pulled into warm, loving hugs.

I wanted to wait a little while before telling them. Perhaps first settling in, but since all the crew are off today and it's only the six of us, I think now would be the best time to come right out and tell them everything.

"Guys, we have something we need to tell you," I say as we walk into the large modern living room. Tay glances at me with questions dancing in her beautiful eyes. She's a gorgeous woman, her face that of glowing happiness when I offer her a wink.

# RYAN

I thought we were going to do this later, but Kierra grabs my hand and we all settle in the living room. "Something I haven't been completely honest about since I met everyone. I've kept it quiet because I didn't want to be treated differently, but…" My girl inhales a calming breath and I offer her hand a squeeze. "My mother died when I was a teenager. She had cancer, the BRCA gene, which is a mutation and it's hereditary. I went home because…"

Her words taper off and she glances at me. Giving her a nod, I bring her hand to my lips, placing a kiss on the smooth skin of her wrist.

"I had my eggs frozen so that when I was ready one day, if the gene was dormant

I wanted to know the option would be there for me to have a child. Also, I had to finally come clean to Mr. Callahan," Kierra grins at me. "I mean I needed to let love in and trust him. I needed to know all was good with my health before committing to Ryan, and also he needed to know what our options are."

"Artificial insemination?" Tayla murmurs the question and Kiki nods.

"And well... I had it done while we were there. The timing had worked out and they were able to complete the insemination. My BRCA gene is dormant, so my doctor recommended we do it and once I got back here, I'll be going for regular checkups."

"Does this mean you're pregnant right now?" This comes from Emma, her eyes alight with excitement.

"Yes." The girls squeal excitedly as they pull Kierra up into warm hugs.

Both Liam and Callum glance at me. And it's then that Cal, the older brother questions. "Are you telling me you're..." He points to Ki, waving his finger up and down. "You're the donor?"

"Yup, Kierra is pregnant with my baby." I tell him proudly. Both brothers rise, shaking my hand. The room is filled with happiness and excitement.

Liam pulls me into a one arm hug and pats me on the back. "You don't do things by half do you? I said put a ring on her finger and you go one step further." He chuckles. "I'm happy for you man. You deserve this. You finally got your girl."

Nodding, I can't help the happiness that grips my heart. "Thank you for pushing me to finally do it. To go get her."

"You would have done it anyway. But I'd like to think I'm responsible for the ring and the baby," he smirks confidently which earns him a swat from Kierra.

"Liam, stop being an ass," she retorts playfully.

Since we got back it's been nothing but work. With the preparations for the upcoming local tour we're about to head off on, we've also been handling the PR nightmare with Tiffany and her claim that the little girl is mine. I'm in the studio when the doorbell goes. Everyone is out and I'm ready to call it a day because Ki and I have plans to go to the beach. Rising from the chair, I head toward the security cameras and find the woman who's claiming me as the father standing at the door.

I make my way to the door and once it opens I'm met with the familiar green eyes of a woman I knew a long time ago. I haven't seen her in years and I still don't remember the night I spent with her. That's the only reason I'm doubting her claims.

"Hi," she says with a smile, one that I don't return.

"What are you doing here? Our lawyers will be in contact with you."

"I know, I just… I got the papers, Ryan. Are you sure you want to put her through that?" She asks, pointing at the little brown-haired girl standing just behind her.

"Ryan, what's going on?" Kierra stands in the doorway and I flit my glance over to Tiffany. Both women stare at me for an answer and I can't give them one. The little girl with hair as dark as mine glances up from behind her mother.

"Mommy, can we go swimming?" The soft voice is enough to turn the pain in my heart into an ache. I drag my eyes back to Ki, anger, frustration, and wariness settle over her beautiful features. I know this is difficult for her, it is for me too.

"Yes, we can go in a moment. Go sit in the car and wait for me." The girl nods and smiles at me, she offers me a wave that I can't return because I'm in shock. As soon as she's back in the car, the tension around us skyrockets.

"There's nothing to say Tiffany. Once the tests come back we can talk, before that, I have nothing to say to you." I inform her, my voice firm and confident.

"I was the one-night stand," she says glancing at Kierra. "I've come to tell Ryan I'll give him the paternity test he asked for." The woman I spent one night with. Stupidity and drunkenness got to me that night and I let go of my inhibitions.

Before I realized I loved Kierra and we had a chance, I did something I may now regret. Not because I could be a father, but because I've finally got the woman I love and this could tear us apart indefinitely.

Kierra grabs my hand, lacing her fingers with mine as if she's showing me that she's with me no matter what. The same way I'm hers no matter what. "I'm the fiancée and I'll be by his side no matter what." Ki affirms with a confidence that makes my heart catapult in my chest. Meeting her stormy eyes, I take in the woman I love.

What she's just confirmed has made me love her even more. No matter what happens, I'll never want another woman. My heart belongs to Kierra Thorne. Soon to be Kierra Callahan. And there's nothing that's going to come between that.

When I drag my gaze back to the woman who is a stranger to me, she nods defeated. "I'm going to get going, thank you Ryan." Tiffany stares at me for a moment, before turning to walk away.

As I follow her out, I lean in when I pass Ki and whisper. "Please wait for me. I'll be back in a sec." She nods slowly, watching the woman walk toward the car.

When I reach Tiffany, she turns to regard me once more. "I just want my daughter to know her father. If that's you, I'd like to make sure she knows you. It's never my intention to come between you and your fiancée." I don't respond, because I can feel her lies dripping from every word. She wants something, I don't know what it is, but I'll find out.

Something tells me that she's hiding a lot more than she's letting on, but If the little girl is mine, I'll make sure she doesn't want for anything. There will never be a day in her life that she feels as if she's not wanted or loved. Two years is a long time to miss out on your child's life, but I hope I get to make it up to her.

Once the tests come back, I'll make my decision. As long as I don't lose the woman I love, I know I'll make it through. I turn and head back to the house to find Ki watching me intently.

"I meant what I said, Ryan. I'm not going anywhere. She can claim as much as she wants, only until those tests come back will we know for sure. Even then, I'm still yours. I'll always be yours." She vows, and I can't help pulling her into my arms and keeping her close. This woman is my everything.

"I love you so much, Kiki. Nothing will take me away from you. I've wanted you and loved you too long to let anything get in the way. It doesn't matter what the outcome is, I'll always be yours. I don't want another woman."

She steps back and regards me with a smile. One that lights up her face. "Then let's go inside and you can show me how much you want me." Mischief dances in those blue orbs and I quickly lift her in my arms and walk her back into the house where I intend on showing her how much I love her in so many different ways she'll be begging for me to stop.

Since the band leaves tomorrow for a gig in New York, I won't see her for three days, I'll need to get my fill, even though I know it's impossible. I'll never get enough of Kierra Thorne.

# KIERRA

It's been three days away. Since Ryan's been on tour, I had the time to get a few checkups done. We've been back for just over a month and I had a feeling about something that's been confirmed. He's going to either be surprised and happy, or completely and utterly shocked. Either way, I can't wait to tell him. "Tay," I call out and when she turns I can't help smiling. Her stomach is round and her face is glowing.

"God, Ki! I thought you'd call. Ryan's been beside himself. Beside the fact that I missed you, the boys were driving me insane asking questions. You do realize you're never to do that to me again. Ever."

I nod. "I promise, but this is the surprise. I couldn't let Ryan see before it's ready," I respond guiltily. As we make our way out of the hospital we head out to the large parking lot. I can see the SUV from where we exit through large sliding doors. I didn't expect any of the guys to pick me up, but somehow, I don't think Callum would have let Tay drive alone. "Who's here?"

"Cal. The other two are recording this afternoon," she murmurs knowing I want to ask about Ryan.

"How is he?"

Nodding, she offers a wry smile. "He's a jumble of emotions to be honest. Worried about you. When you made me promise not to tell him about everything, I kept my vow, but it was difficult to see him like that." She answers honestly. I had to keep this a secret until I knew I'd be able to pull it off. Even though I shouldn't have gone alone, but it was the only way to get everything ready. When I walked out of the meeting I knew it would be okay. All of it would work out. Now all I have to do is show Ryan. Hopefully he'll forgive me for disappearing for two days. I had a feeling about it, but when I went in to

166

see Dr. Scholie she confirmed my suspicions.

We reach the car and Cal jumps out, pulling me into a fierce hug. His arms are warm, affectionate. "Ki," he murmurs into my hair. Releasing me, he regards me with those big blue eyes. "Are you okay?"

"I'm fine. I told Tay it will all be okay and I had to set up this surprise alone or you and Liam would have blabbed about it. I just couldn't look at him if this doesn't work." He eyes me warily, then nods.

"Just don't go disappearing like that. Even though it's only for two days. If Tay had done that to me, I'd have put her over my lap and spanked her ass." A huff comes from the blonde beauty.

"You'd like to think you would. Can we go? Before we get the paparazzi freaking out." She questions with her narrowed gaze on her husband. Callum nods and smiles.

"Yeah, let's get Ki back to her man before he cuts my balls off." Callum helps me with the small bag and ushers his wife into the passenger seat.

"So? Are you going to tell me before

you tell him?" Tay's inquisitive gaze meets mine in the rear mirror. I know she's dying to know.

Shrugging, I regard her. "It is. I was right."

"Oh my God!" Her screech is so loud, Callum jumps into the driver's seat.

"What the fuck is going on?"

"Nothing, Tayla was just saying the baby kicked," I lie, and Callum knows it. We've known each other for far too long for him to buy my lies. And to be honest, it's difficult to lie to the man. His sky-blue gaze penetrates me, and I find myself needing to turn away.

Sighing, he starts the car and pulls out into the traffic. Thankfully the conversation shifts from my news to the upcoming tour that the boys are playing across the country. I'll be going with them, but Tay has been told she's staying home. With her so far along, I think it's best, and she'll have Emma to be there if she needs anything.

Since it's not an international tour, Callum has agreed to do it, only if he can fly home if the baby comes. Which is understandable since he's a first-time father. The thought of seeing Ryan again and telling him what I found out will be interesting. I don't doubt he'll be excited, but I'm still nervous. As the silence settles around us, I watch the city pass by as we head to Cal's house.

Once we pull up to the drive, before I have time to get out of the car, I'm met with the piercing glare of Ryan Callahan. My soon-to-be husband, the father of my future children, and the man who looks like he wants to spank me until I cry out his name in apology.

"Where the fuck have you been, baby? I missed you so much. What was with your no calls rule?"

"Can we talk inside?" I question, without thinking, he reaches for me. Shielding me from everyone, he tugs me along with him as we enter the house. Ignoring the crew, Liam and Emma, he tugs me into the piano room and shuts the door.

"Talk." With his arms folded, he watches me with a severe expression.

"I stayed overnight at the hospital. They did a checkup, but…" my words taper off. My heart races, slamming against my chest.

"Kierra, if you don't tell me what the fuck is going on, I'm going to lose—"

"It's twins." I blurt out before he can say anything more. His words are halted, his eyes grow wide with shock as he watches me.

"What?"

"We're having twins." Lifting my shirt, I show him the lipstick drawing I made on my belly. It's stupid, but I thought it would be perfect for revealing the surprise. "I was worried, so I stayed overnight, but it was merely just to make sure we're all healthy. I didn't take you with because I wanted to surprise you."

"Fuck," he growls, pulling me into his arms. The heat of him cocoons me. "Don't ever fucking do that again. Next time you go for a checkup, you take me with. I don't care how far I have to travel back." He's right, but they were away filming a video and of course came back early and he found out I wasn't home. Poor Tayla had to deal with this grumpy ass.

"You were busy. I couldn't interrupt—" his mouth crashes to mine silencing my words. Twining my arms around his neck, I tug him closer, needing him to consume me. Whenever we're apart I feel alone, empty, even when he's only a couple of towns away, I miss him like he's a part of me.

# RYAN

"Twins." The word still feels foreign on my tongue. Two babies.

"You don't do things by half measure do you, man?" Liam chuckles, regarding me with happiness. "Actually, you do them by double measure!" He guffaws, slapping me on the back in camaraderie, which only earns him a glare from his wife.

He's known me for far too long not to realize how much this means to me. Since he first noticed the way I looked at Kierra at one of our first meetings, he never stopped his bullshit. For more than too long he's told me to *go for it*. To be honest. Now that I finally have done it, I couldn't be happier. She's finally accepted that I'm not going anywhere.

"Seriously, Liam. You're not that funny, at least not all the time." Emma quips, lifting her brow in a high arch as she regards my best friend.

"Baby, you didn't say that last night when I—"

"Okay! I do NOT need to be scarred right now," I grunt, pushing up from the sofa. We've just finished our meeting with Kierra and Callum about the world tour coming up next year. It takes a lot to organize, but we've all agreed we're outsourcing everything. I don't want my woman working long hours when she's pregnant.

*I am as bad as Callum.*

"Ryan." Turning to regard Liam, he waits for me to respond to a question I didn't hear. "I asked if you wanted to order in? Emm and I are thinking of calling delivery."

"Yeah, sure. I'm going to head into the music room. I've got something to finish." With that, I walk out, leaving them to decide on dinner. Me, on the other hand, I've got something special to work on. Making my way up toward the music room which houses the piano, I stalk past the kitchen where Callum and Kierra are talking about the venue options for next year.

Since we're doing four acoustic shows, set up will be different and we'll also need permission if we're playing in the church in Paris. It's a beautiful old building which allows for brilliant acoustics.

My plan is to sit down and finish the song I'd been writing for Ki. She doesn't know about it yet, but when I play it, I know she'll never forget about our journey. Pushing open the door, I step inside and lock myself inside.

Stepping into the offices of Howard and Associates, I've got Kierra's hand firmly grasped in mine. This is it, the moment of truth. "It's going to be okay, you know?" Turning my gaze on Ki, I can't help but feel my heart fill with love for her. I'm meant to be giving her support, yet here she is showing me more than I could ever possibly want or need.

The emotion in her eyes is clear. She's here no matter what the outcome of this meeting is. It won't change a thing between us. I'll marry her, she'll be my partner for life, and if it means we have another little girl to care for, then so be it.

Honestly, I'm nervous. Not because I might be a father already, but because I don't know how I'd handle having a child I may only see on weekends, or perhaps won't have a chance to watch grow up. Something tells me Tiffany isn't going to be forthcoming with allowing me into her daily life.

"Mr. Callahan, nice to see you again," Peter, our lawyer rises from his seat when we walk into the boardroom.

"Good to see you, Mr. Howard." We shake hands, then he offers Kierra a warm smile. They've been our legal assistance since the band formed ten years ago. I trust them with everything I have.

"Take a seat, I received the results this morning from the hospital and I'm sure opposing counsel has as well. Look Ryan, I can't really tell you what the right thing to do is, but we'll make sure you're safe from any slander." His serious tone makes my chest tighten with anxiety. Just then, Kierra pushes up and rushes out the door. It only takes me a second to race after her and right into the ladies' room which is thankfully empty.

"Baby, Kiki, are you okay?" She's in the stall and I can't do anything about it, unless I break the damn door down.

"Just give me a minute, Ryan."

I can tell she's crying. I know this woman so well I can pick up on the slightest change in her demeanor. This can't be easy for her, I just wish I could lessen the tension. When the stall door opens and Kierra steps out, her eyes are bloodshot. "Baby," she allows me to pull her into my arms. Her body shakes and I know she's crying.

"I'm sorry, just… I'm overly emotional." I step away from her, lifting her chin so I can look into those stormy eyes.

"Never be sorry. It's difficult, I know I've put you in this position, but I'm yours.

You're mine. This is a formality, Ki. It doesn't matter what happens in there, I'm not letting you walk out of my life." She nods, and I can't help planting a soft kiss on her lips. "Now let's go find out the results."

Walking down the hall toward the meeting room has the tension hanging thick in the air. Once we step inside, Mr. Howard offers a nod. "I doubt Ms. Edwards and her lawyer will be much longer and we can then go ahead with the findings." He's right, it's not long when Tiffany walks in followed by an older gentleman who looks like he's ready to go into battle. Her daughter isn't with her, which makes me wonder where the little girl is.

Once all the pleasantries are out of the way, Mr. Howard offers me the envelope. "You're welcome to open that and we'll go into more detail with what's going to happen with the result." My hand trembles when I lift the white package from the dark wood table. My heart catapults into my throat with anxiousness. I don't know what I want it to be. A negative or positive.

"I... I just hope it's what you want. If she is yours, I don't want you to feel as if you need to do anything or be there. If you don't want to of course." Tiffany murmurs from across the table. I bristle at her words. Ripping the envelope open, I pull the pages out and inhale a deep breath. When my gaze scans over the words I have to read and re read them. Lifting my gaze, I meet hers. The stranger before me.

Without a word, I slide the envelope along with the pages over to her and the lawyer seated beside her. My emotions are all over the place. Skittering down my spine is a shiver of confusion.

I knew it. I felt it in my gut.

It was something I'd wanted, but not. The one emotion I find at the forefront is relief.

I'm not the father. She's not mine.

"I'm sorry Ryan. This has been... I'm just sorry." The woman says to me, but I can't look at her. I'm not sure why. I've never been one for anger, but right now, I feel it.

"Why did you do this?" I question,

spinning to face her. Guilt flashes over her features. Her gaze drops, it's dark and guarded. "Just tell me something before you go. What made you wait two years to come to me? You could have told me when you found out you were pregnant. This is something that could ruin my career. Is it personal gain?"

"I needed help and I thought if I could find her father he could help me financially. I wasn't sure who the father was. There were two men I knew it could be, you being one of them. I didn't do it to hurt you." She sighs then, lifting her gaze to mine. "I just wanted my daughter to know her father."

"And I'm not him." My words are terse, filled with anger. Pushing up, I shake my lawyers hand, "I need air." Stalking out of the boardroom, I find a quiet spot near the terrace that's situated near the exit. The view of the Hollywood hills greets me and I can't help wondering what would have happened if it was my child. I can't let that thought in right now. There's only one woman who needs me and she's got me, all of me.

"Ryan, are you okay?" Kierra's soft tone comes from behind me.

"I am." Turning, I meet her gaze dead on. "I'm not the father." Her smile is bright, the tension that surrounded her only moments ago has dissipated and I can't help feeling the happiness that this woman brings into my life. "We can move on without anything in the way. It's us, no one else." She smiles then, wrapping her arms around my waist, I lean in and inhale her scent. Sweet, like a dessert I'll never tire of tasting. Mine.

# KIERRA

"Ryan, you're being ridiculous. I'm not even showing yet." His glare is enough to scare the crew, but this is me. I don't back down. Not from anyone. Including the man I love.

"You're going to take time off. I just want to you get through this first trimester."

"And what do you know about getting through this? You're a man." Crossing my arms in front of my chest, I meet his glare with one of my own. He's going to be as bad as Callum.

"I've Googled." He retorts indignantly.

"Ugh, you're insufferable," turning, I head into the studio to grab my laptop. He's not going to stop me from at least sending out our marketing emails, as well as sorting out the hotels for the next few shows.

"Baby," his voice is low behind me, but I don't turn around. I feel his body heat behind me and before I know it, his arms are wrapped around me. His big hands splay on my belly as he circles it with the gentlest of touches. "I just want you and the babies safe and healthy."

"I know Ryan, but I can still do my job." Turning in his arms, I meet his gaze that's filled with so much love I'm breathless.

"I want to show you something. Sit down," he gestures to the sofa, then makes his way to the keyboard that's set up for the recording session later.

"What are you doing?" Furrowing my brow, I watch him settle behind the instrument. When those dark eyes pierce me with a stare that's filled with amusement, I can't help wondering what he's hiding up his sleeve.

"Just listen," he murmurs, then starts playing.

*Friends turn to lovers,*

*Fragile turns to forever,*
*I chose you,*
*I want you*

*Between want and fear,*
*I need you more,*
*No more what ifs,*
*No more another time,*
*Because it's ours*
*Between want and fear*
*You're mine now*

*Maybe turns to Yes,*
*You've given me all,*
*Release your fear,*
*You want me too*

*Between want and fear,*
*I need you more,*
*No more what ifs,*
*No more another time,*
*Because it's ours*
*Between want and fear*
*You're mine now*

When he stops I can't breathe. My heart is erratic, beating its way from my chest wanting to mold itself to his. "Ryan, I…"

"It's something small. I don't normally write, but…" He shrugs, then meets my teary gaze. "I wanted to tell you how much I love you in words. In a song that will be immortalized forever." He rises from the piano stool and reaches for my hands.

"You're amazing. I'm sorry it took me so long to let you in. I've always been scared. Losing someone I love isn't something I'd ever want to go through again. Losing you, I'm not sure I'd survive it." I tell him honestly.

"I'll always be here, baby. For you and our babies." Leaning up on my tip toes, I crash my lips to his earning me a low growl. His hands trail down my hips, gripping the cheeks of my ass, he lifts me up against his body. Walking us back toward the desk, he sits me down settling himself between my legs.

"Ryan, we can't in here…" I whisper when he finally breaks the kiss.

"Baby, I'll worship your body anywhere I want. Sit back, and spread those pretty legs. I'm starving and I'd like to devour my soon-to-be wife's sweet pussy." He growls with a low rumble as he places hands on my thighs, splaying them. "Such pretty panties," he murmurs as he slides the material to the side.

"Ryan, we—"

"Shh, baby, all I want to do is eat you until you're screaming. So, the only words that are going to be falling from those rosy lips will be my name, or *"oh God more, Ryan"*. Is that understood?"

I nod. I can't find words to respond when his mouth then crashes down on my core, lapping and licking at the arousal that's just for him. His fingers tease, his tongue taunts, and his warm breath has me teetering on the edge suddenly needing release.

The man completely consumes me. He feasts until I'm shuddering, gripping his hair tugging him closer as my hips undulate against his face and my cries echo around us. And as he ordered, it's his name that the whole house has now heard me screaming at the top of my lungs.

*My man.*

*My love.*

*My forever.*

# EPILOGUE

"Cal, can I take the stage after the show?" One of my best friend's turns to regard me with questions in his eyes. I know what he's thinking and he'll be right to assume. There's something I've been wanting to do for too long and I'm tired of waiting around.

Both of them are married with kids on the way. It's time I start my own family. And today is that day. "Sure, you going to finally do it?" He questions and I nod. "Good man. I'm happy for you, but enough sappy shit, let's get down to sound check and get this show on the road."

The walk to stage doesn't get easier, there's always nerves that get the better of me, but when we round the corner, Kierra's gray blue eyes meet mine and all the fear and anxiety that plagues me is gone. Her presence calms me and I know I can and have to do this.

"Boys, are we ready? Can I get the fans in for sound check?" I nod, pulling her into my arms and inhale her scent which reminds me of apple pie. Sweet cinnamon which has my taste buds watering to taste her again.

"Can you two keep your hands off each other for twenty minutes?" Liam comes strolling onto the stage with his drumsticks. The cocky mouth of my best friend is ever present and I can't help chuckling.

He and Emma are just the same, they're constantly sucking face. It's like an overload of PDA that will make anyone puke.

"Shut it. Get ready, let's do this." My retort is met with a raised brow and a smirk as he eyes me and Kierra.

"I'm ready, man. This is Liam fucking Hayes you're talking to; I was born ready." With that confident comment, he swaggers up to the raised platform where his drum set sits and settles on the stool.

"I'll see you after the show, baby." Ki,

leans up on her tiptoes and plants a soft kiss on my lips.

Her sweet smile is enough to make my night, but I've got a show to play. She turns to walk away, but before she disappears with Tay, she regards me over her shoulder. "Knock 'em dead, handsome."

Making my way to the platform, I find my keyboard set up along with the microphone. "We ready?" Callum bounds to the front of the stage and the girls that are entering the venue start screaming. I don't know how he handles being the center of all that attention and keeps it from harming his marriage.

He's always been popular with the ladies, thankfully I've managed to keep myself mostly in the shadows. He turns to give me the nod and I start the song Liam wrote for Emma.

The keyboards are easy and I watch as Cal entrances the girls with his voice.

*One night, one kiss*
*One touch, one smile*

*You've haunted me,*
*Taunted me, but always made me feel*

*Between lust & tears,*
*We found our way*
*The path isn't easy,*
*But you're my salvation*
*Between lust & tears*

*Now it's forever,*
*Just me and you,*
*Fire and ice,*
*Passion and love*

*Between lust & tears,*
*We found our way*
*The path wasn't easy,*
*But you're my salvation*
*Between lust & tears*

The show has been incredible and the energy from the crowd have pushed me through. Exhaustion is slowly getting the better of me, but I know tonight is special, so before we leave the stage, Callum makes his announcements. "Now, before we leave you, Ryan wanted to say a few words. You see, my best friend has fallen in love. He's found his forever and I think he's going to say something."

I'm a flurry of fucking nerves because this is it. I've never wanted more anything in my life. Not even landing the gig with Hunters made me feel like this. So excited. So needy. Jesus, I sound like a woman. "Thanks, man," I rasp as Cal hands me the microphone.

"Hey guys, thanks for coming out and making this show amazing," my words have the crowd going wild. Raising my hand, I motion for them to simmer down, which they do. "Now, you all know my best friends have both found their forever, Callum being married, and Liam on his way there soon enough, I figured, you know… It's my turn."

Glancing behind me, I notice Ki standing in the shadows. She's never been one for the public eye, but this time she has no choice.

"I'm here tonight, to tell you about my girl, Kierra," I turn my glance toward her and crook my finger. "Come out here." When she strolls over to me, I can't help grinning like a kid on Christmas morning counting my lucky stars this woman loves me too.

The crowd are silent as they watch her step on stage. All our fans know who she is, and even though we've always been behind the scenes, I want to shout it out to the world. Letting them know she's mine. That this woman has agreed to marry me.

"Now, this woman has put up with my crazy lifestyle, she's been there since the beginning and she's still here. The announcement I wanted to make this evening is to tell you all, our fans who've been supporting us for so long, that Kierra has agreed to marry me, and that's not all. To top that, we're having twins. And as much as I know I'm embarrassing her," I smile, grasping her hand in mine. "Ki, I love you, I've always loved you. Without you, my life wasn't complete, but with you, I know my song will play forever." Swooning comes from the crowd and a few whistles and catcalls.

Those blue eyes that sparkle with excitement, are glistening with unshed tears. She takes the microphone from me and turns to the crowd. "Thank you for everything. Your support and love have given the band more than fans, you've given us a family. As much as I do stay behind the scenes, I'd like you all to know, Ryan and I will be getting married before the tour next year." That's when the crowd goes wild.

Then, she nods, her words slowly settle on me and my heart rate skyrockets with happiness. She fucking knocked me on my ass once again. Since the first time I met her, she's always kept me on my toes, and this time it's no different. Lifting her, I spin her around and the crowd is absolutely crazy— they're shouting and screaming. Then I feel the arms of my brothers, the men who've stood by me for so long.

And I feel the emotion I've longed for.

True happiness.

This is what it feels like.

And there's nothing more I want in this world.

She's here. In my arms.

And she's going to be my wife.

# PLAYLIST

It Will Rain - Bruno Mars
Beautiful - Alyssa Reid
Fast Car - Jasmine Thompson
Eyes on Fire - Blue Foundation
It's All Games - Kristina Maria
All I Ever Want is You - Megan Davies
Hurts - Emeli Sandé
Silhouette - Aquilo
I Want Crazy - Hunter Hayes
Grand Piano - Nicki Minaj

Find full playlist on Spotify

.

# BONUS EXCERPT

CALLUM

Backstage Series Book #1

(Callum & Tayla)

# PROLOGUE

When you're the man every woman wants, the one they would drop their panties for in a heartbeat, no questions asked,

What do you do?

I do what every other red-blooded man does. I take advantage. But what happens when you find one woman who changes the way you feel about yourself? Your life? And your heart?

Do you recognize the moment your life changes?

When you find clarity?

When the constant confusion you have becomes an untangled ball of string? The notes that are caught in your head for days on end suddenly play in an exquisitely constructed symphony.

That's what happened the day I laid eyes on her. When she slammed into me, spilling her milky cappuccino over my favorite white T-shirt.

When chestnut eyes and sleek ice-blonde hair invaded my senses. Her sweet vanilla perfume engulfed my veins, and all I could see was the delicate angel.

My name is Callum Hayes.

I am a rock star, a rock god.

The tabloids call me a bad boy. They write the articles I want them to write. The image I portray is one of sex and rock 'n' roll. Aren't rock stars meant to do that?

I'm sitting in my music room. The only place I can be myself. The real me nobody else sees. Images rush through my mind of what I crave to do to that gorgeous woman, distracting me from what I'm supposed to be doing.

Writing.

The want I feel for her is primal. I ache to bend her over this fucking piano, pull her tight little panties down her toned legs, and sink myself so deep inside that sexy little body, ruining her for any other man. I need her sweet pussy to mold only to my cock.

I want to make her yearn and ache for my mouth on her. My fingers inside her and my cock claiming her. Today was Tayla's second official day with us. She's got an ear for music and sound, which led her here, to our recording studio I set up in our home.

She's my brother's sound engineer, helping him set up the drum kit, aiding the other techs with tuning the guitars, and today, I've asked her to do mine. Nobody touches my baby, but I've allowed this beauty to lay her fingers on the instrument. She'll soon be on tour with us, and I can't wait to get her backstage.

My mind has been filled with dirty images since her interview. I turn my attention to the notebook. The words are jumbled, like the muddle in my mind. She will be the death of me. If I can't have her, I don't know what I'll do. Liam, my brother, is right. I put myself in situations like this, but this time feels different.

The way her cheeky mouth challenges me makes me wish to see how much I can challenge her.

There is one thing he's mistaken about though. Tayla Quinn will be mine.

Beneath me. Writhing. Moaning. Whimpering. Begging.

When I take her and make her scream my name, she'll ache only for me.

Callum fucking Hayes.

# THANK YOU

There's always that one book, the one that is elusive for so long you think it will never come. And then, when it does, you're blown away by the support.

Readers, I know you've been waiting on Ryan and Kierra for such a long time, but thank you for not giving up on me. In believing that he was waiting on his story to be told at the right time.

My Alpha BETAs who loved Ryan as much as I have—Becca, Tamara, Melissa, and Cat. Thank you for reading this story from it's first draft to the final proof.

The Street Team, you ladies work your ass off to get my name out there, thank you! Tre, Tam, Becca, Sheena, Susan, Sarah, and the rest of the ladies, from the bottom of my little black heart, THANK YOU!

My Darklings!! This group is like my own personal form of therapy. Thank you!! There is never a dull moment, and that's what makes me thankful for your love and support. It's not easy working with the intense stress and deadlines, but you always seem to brighten my day!

To my fellow authors who are there with advice, support, and just a general pick me up. Thank you. It means more to me than you know. Thank you for sharing my work with your readers, and giving me a friendship that is second to none.

To the bloggers, you ladies read, read, read, support, post, review, and you do it with a smile. Thank you!! We wouldn't be here if it weren't for you, so keep what you're doing, we appreciate you! #AllBlogsMatter!

Lastly, to the readers, thank YOU! It's because of you I'm able to put out book after book. Giving you what you ask for, and hopefully making you excited about the next book. Thank you for your reviews, keeping them SPOILER FREE ;) But most of all, thank you for buying our books. For your support, love, and encouragement.

THANK YOU!
D x

# ABOUT DANI

Dani is a *USA Today* bestselling author of a variety of genres, from romantic suspense to dark erotic romance and even BDSM romance. She loves to delve into the raw, emotional journeys her characters venture on, and enjoys the dark, edgy, and sensual scenes that fill the pages of her books. Dani's stories are seductive with a deviant edge with feisty heroines and dominant alphas.

Dani lives in the beautiful city of Cape Town, and is a proud member of the Romance Writer's Organization of South Africa (ROSA) and the Romance Writers of America (RWA). She has a healthy addiction to reading, TV series, music, tattoos, chocolate, and ice cream.

www.danirene.com
info@danirene.com

# OTHER BOOKS

### *Stand Alones*
*Choosing the Hart*
*Love Beyond Words*
*Cuffed*
*Fragile Innocence*
*Perfectly Flawed*
*Black Light: Obsessed*
*Among Ash and Ember*
*Within Me (Limited Time)*
*Cursed in Love (collaboration with Cora Kenborn)*
*Beautifully Brutal (Cavalieri Della Morte)*

### *Taboo Novellas*
*Sunshine and the Stalker (collaboration with K Webster)*
*His Temptation*

*Austin's Christmas Shortcake*
*Crime and Punishment (Newsletter Exclusive)*
*Malignus (Inferno World Novella)*
*Virulent (collaboration with Yolanda Olson)*
*Tempting Grayson*

### Sins of Seven Series
*Kneel (Book #1)*
*Obey (Book #2)*
*Indulge (Book #3)*
*Ruthless (Book #4)*
*Bound (Book #5)*
*Envy (Book #6)*
*Vice (Book #7)*

### The Stolen Series
*Stolen*
*Severed*
*TBC*

### Four Fathers Series
*Kingston*

### Four Sons Series
*Brock*

www.ingramcontent.com/pod-product-compliance
Lightning Source LLC
Chambersburg PA
CBHW070747180626
46818CB00007B/3018